THORNS
OF THE VEIL

BOOK ONE OF THE VEILBOUND SAGA

By Eira Blackthorn

MK STORYWORKS

First published in 2025 by MK Storyworks.

ISBN: 978-1-80700-031-8

Dedication

To the rebels of the mundane, the alchemists who distill wonder from the dust motes dancing in sunbeams, to the silent gladiators locked in brutal duels against demons only they can perceive, and to the lovers whose very souls hum with the forgotten melodies of a world that calls to them across the void this saga bleeds for you.

For every fractured spirit that has known the agonizing siren song of a destiny far more vast, far more terrifying than the cage of their current existence. For those whose eyes, blazing with an unquenchable thirst, have dared to pry open the tightly sealed lids of the ordinary and felt the primal, seismic tremors of something **more**.

May you, with a heart thundering against your ribs, find your own elusive Fae prince lurking in the deepest, most intoxicating shadows. May your dormant power a sleeping leviathan awaken with the violent, bleeding dawn. May you unearth the raw, unyielding courage to shatter the brittle walls of the known and step, trembling but resolute, into the terrifying embrace of the unknown.

To my own burning constellation of muses, the unwavering anchors who champion the impossible, whose defiant faith ignites the very stars in my sky: my blood, my chosen kin, and the luminous tapestry of souls **you**, my readers, who breathe fire and starlight into these crumbling, wondrous realms. Your ravenous passion is the fuel that roars through my pen; your fierce encouragement, the tempest that lifts my wings.

And to the guttural groans of ancient, slumbering forests; the cryptic, luminous pronouncements of the night sky; and the untamed, all-consuming heart of magic itself my deepest, most resonant thanks for the epic tales you eternally weave. May this plunge into the *Veilbound Saga* be merely the first thunderous collision of our shared adventures.

Author's Note

Hey there, wonderful readers!

This story, *Thorns of the Veil*, is for all the dreamers who feel their magic bubbling just beneath the surface, and for those who've been silenced when their souls were made for roaring storms.

It began as a soft whisper a thought about love that dares to defy destiny, power that demands a steep price, and a young woman who discovers that survival isn't about giving in, but about finding a fierce, different kind of strength.

Elara's journey is a beautifully tangled thread of pain, fury, tenderness, and courage because all those emotions have the right to exist together. It's a reminder that you can carry your shadows and still reach for the light.

If you've ever been told you're too much, too wild, or too broken, I hope this story reminds you that you are, in fact, exactly enough.

Thank you for bravely stepping through the Veil with me. Just know this story is only the beginning.

Eira Blackthorn

TABLE OF CONTENTS

Chapter 1

Oakhaven. The name itself conjured images of ancient oaks, their gnarled branches reaching like arthritic fingers toward a perpetually overcast sky. It was a village cradled in the gentle embrace of rolling hills, a place where time seemed to amble rather than march. For Elara, it was home. A home that smelled of drying herbs, of woodsmoke clinging to damp earth, and of the faint, persistent sweetness of her grandmother's lavender sachets.

Her days followed a quiet rhythm dictated by her grandmother, Maeve. The old woman's breath had grown shallow over the past months, and her eyes, though milky with age, seemed to see far beyond the physical world. Maeve was the village's keeper of lore, a woman whose wisdom was sought when omens were dire. Each morning, Elara would rise with the sun to brew her grandmother's herbal teas, meticulously measure tinctures, and read aloud from worn volumes of village history.

The whispers, however, were a constant undercurrent to the mundane. They spoke of the Veil. Not the thin, gauzy fabric of a summer morning, but a shimmering, ethereal boundary that separated their familiar world from something else entirely. It lay just beyond the whispering woods that skirted Oakhaven, a place where the trees grew taller, the shadows deepened, and the air itself seemed to vibrate with an unseen energy. Villagers told of lights dancing at its edge on moonless nights, of strange music carried on the wind, and of the chilling cold that settled upon the land when the Veil was particularly active.

Elara had grown up with these tales, yet for her there was something more. A subtle hum beneath her skin, a faint resonance that no one else seemed to perceive. It was like a silent song played only for her, a vibration that thrummed in her bones when she neared the edge of the woods. She often found herself drawn there, her gaze drifting toward the distant shimmer that marked the Veil's boundary.

One afternoon, as the sun began its slow descent and painted the sky in hues of rose and gold, Elara wandered deeper into the woods than usual. She was searching for moonpetal, a rare herb prized for its healing properties and luminous petals. Her grandmother used it in tinctures for deep wounds and persistent fevers. The air grew cooler as she walked, the village sounds faded, and the Veil felt closer here. Its subtle hum grew more pronounced with each step.

She saw it then. A tear no larger than a robin's egg shimmered into existence before her. It was a fleeting rift, a momentary warp in the smooth expanse of the Veil. Through its infinitesimal opening spilled a cascade of light, not the harsh glare of sun but a soft, iridescent glow that carried the very essence of starlight. With the light came a melody, faint and haunting, like the echo of a forgotten lullaby.

Through the ephemeral portal, she glimpsed a figure. Tall and slender, cloaked in shadows that seemed woven from moonlight and twilight, he exuded a chilling grace. His features were sharp, shaped by an artistry unknown to mortal hands. His eyes were pools of molten silver, holding ancient wisdom and profound sorrow in their depths.

The vision vanished as quickly as it appeared, the tear sealing with a silent sigh. Elara stood breathless and trembling in the deepening twilight, the scent of moonpetal forgotten. Her heart hammered against her ribs as she stared at the spot where the rift had been, half convinced she'd imagined it all.

That evening, the cottage air was thick with dried herbs and something else. Something sharp and metallic, like the tang of lightning before a storm. Elara delivered the few moonpetals she had managed to gather; her hands still unsteady. Maeve's piercing gaze settled on her the moment she entered.

"The Veil whispers to you, child," Maeve said, her voice a dry rustle of leaves. "I have seen it in your eyes and felt it in the earth beneath your feet."

Elara froze, her heart leaping to her throat.

"You saw something." Maeve stated it as fact, not question. "The air is disturbed."

"A light," Elara whispered. "A person. His eyes were silver."

Maeve's face grew grave, the lines deepening around her mouth. "There are prophecies," she continued, her voice low and careful. "Fragments of forgotten songs that speak of those who can bridge the divide. Those with the gift, or perhaps the burden, to touch the edges of the unseen."

She reached out a gnarled hand and clasped Elara's wrist with surprising strength. "The Veil is fragile, child, and what lies beyond is not always benevolent. That you have seen him... it is an omen. Draw no undue attention to yourself. Ancient pacts were made long ago, and ancient powers do not sleep forever. The world beyond the Veil watches, and it hungers."

Her words settled like a stone in Elara's stomach. The conversation lingered long after, planting a seed of foreboding in the fertile ground of Elara's growing connection to the world beyond.

The following nights were restless. Maeve's warning echoed

in Elara's mind, mingling with the haunting melody and the silver gaze of the being she'd glimpsed beyond the Veil. The hum beneath her skin became a persistent thrum, a constant reminder of unseen forces at work.

On a night when the moon was a mere sliver and the stars seemed to burn with desperate intensity, the shadow fell over Oakhaven. It wasn't a passing cloud but a presence, a palpable chill that seeped into the land's very marrow. Crickets fell silent. An unnatural quiet descended over the village like a held breath.

From the edge of the woods, a figure emerged. He moved with unnatural fluidity, a silent predator gliding through the dark. An aura of cold, ancient power preceded him, raising the hairs on Elara's arms even from a distance. Village dogs fell quiet, their barks replaced by whimpers of fear. He paused at the edge of the forest, tilting his head as if listening to something only he could hear. Then his silver eyes, the same haunting eyes she had glimpsed through the rift, swept over Oakhaven's humble dwellings.

He was seeking someone.

His gaze locked onto their cottage.

Elara watched from the window, a knot of fear tightening in her chest. He moved toward them with terrible purpose, his presence radiating tangible cold. Her heart pounded a frantic rhythm as the door creaked open at his silent command, revealing him fully in the lamplight.

His face, framed by the hood of his dark cloak, was etched with a weariness that belied his regal bearing. A face carved by time and burdened by centuries, yet profoundly beautiful in its otherworldly perfection. His silver eyes met hers across the room. There was no overt menace in them, only overwhelming desperation.

"Elara of Oakhaven." His voice was a low, resonant baritone, smooth as polished obsidian and just as dark. "I am Kaelen, Prince of the Unseelie Fae."

The title hung heavy in the air. Unseelie Fae. Creatures of shadow and power, beings from the old stories meant to frighten children into obedience.

Kaelen stepped fully inside, his movement stirring the air with a faint shimmer of magic. He closed the door behind him, muffling the sounds of the night. "I come to you not with threats, but with a plea. A plea born of desperation and necessity."

He spoke then of a curse, an ancient affliction that had plagued his bloodline for generations. Not a physical malady, but a slow decay of their innate magic, a creeping madness that threatened to consume them all. It was a shadow clinging to his lineage, threatening to unravel the very fabric of the Faewild itself.

"I have sensed you, Elara," Kaelen confessed, his voice tinged with a vulnerability that resonated with the hum she felt within herself. "Your connection to the Veil is unlike any other mortal I have encountered. You possess a resonance, an ability to touch its currents that is exceedingly rare and utterly vital. It is this ability I desperately need."

He extended a hand toward her, long-fingered and elegant. "My people falter under this curse. It grows stronger with each passing season. There is no other in the mortal realm who can offer the key to its undoing, no other who possesses the power to help restore balance. I offer you my protection, my aid, and the resources of my court if you agree to help me break this ancient curse."

His gaze intensified, silver eyes burning with barely restrained emotion. "Will you lend me your aid, Elara of Oakhaven? Will you help me save my people and, perhaps in doing so, save your own world from the chaos that will surely follow if the Faewild falls?"

The weight of his words settled on Elara's shoulders, heavy and disorienting. A Fae prince standing in her cottage. A centuries-old curse. A desperate plea for her help. Her simple, quiet world had just been shattered, and she had no idea how to put the pieces back together.

Chapter 2

The weight of Kaelen's words settled upon Elara like a shroud woven from starlight and shadows. The sheer audacity of his revelation, that she might hold the key to breaking a curse plaguing an immortal Fae prince, was almost comical in its impossibility. Her mind struggled to grasp the magnitude of it. It was as if a sparrow had been told it possessed the strength to fell an ancient oak. Disbelief warred with gnawing fear, a cold tendril that wrapped itself around her heart and squeezed the breath from her lungs.

"But how?" The question escaped her lips as a whisper, fragile in the charged atmosphere of the cottage. She looked at Maeve, seeking answers in her grandmother's weathered face. "How can I possibly possess such power? I've never even wielded a broom with any conviction, let alone the fate of realms."

A nervous tremor ran through her hands, and she clasped them together as if to contain the energy thrumming beneath her skin. The world had tilted on its axis. The Fae prince's presence, so potent and alien, had left an indelible mark on her spirit and perception of reality. Every rustle of leaves outside, every creak of the floorboards now seemed to carry hidden meaning, a hint of unseen forces that had carelessly brushed against her life.

Maeve's gaze softened, reflecting a deep well of understanding. She reached out, her weathered hand gently covering Elara's trembling ones. "The Veil, child," she said, her voice steady and calm, "does not discriminate based on our perceived station. It responds to resonance, to a unique alignment of spirit and energy. You have always possessed a rare gift, Elara. A deep, innate connection to the lifeblood of the world around you. The plants whisper their secrets to you. The earth hums its ancient songs beneath your feet. That connection, child, is a form of magic. Kaelen, with his Fae sight, has merely recognized what has always been there, waiting for the right moment to awaken."

Elara pulled her hands away, fresh unease washing over her. "A catalyst? You mean him? His appearance? But that feels wrong. Like a nightmare I can't wake from."

The image of Kaelen's silver eyes flickered in her mind. Ancient. Weary. Yet there had been genuine desperation in them, a raw vulnerability that pierced through her fear. It hadn't been the calculating glint of a predator, but the plea of a soul in torment. That anguish was what lent an unsettling credibility to his claims. Pure malice would have been easier to dismiss. But his desperation felt real, tangible.

"The Veil is a place of immense power, Elara," Maeve continued, her voice a steadying balm to Elara's frayed nerves. "Sometimes its energies bleed into our world. The tear Kaelen spoke of is not merely a fissure between realms. It is a wound, a disruption that allows these energies to flow more freely. You stumbled upon it, child. You saw what you were not meant to see, and in doing so, you became entwined with its fate. Your sensitivity, your unique connection, made you a beacon. A point of focus for its wild magic. Kaelen did not create this potential within you. He merely recognized it and sought to harness it. The curse he carries, the blight upon his bloodline, is intrinsically linked to the instability of the Veil. And you, Elara, are now part of that equation."

Elara hugged herself, the familiar wool of her dress offering little comfort against the internal chill. "But what if I can't? What if I fail? He offered power, protection, but what if I'm not strong enough to wield either? What if I break under the strain?"

The thought of being responsible for such monumental forces paralyzed her. Her life had been a series of small, manageable tasks: tending her grandmother's garden, brewing soothing teas, learning to identify medicinal herbs. This was an entirely different realm, a world of gods and monsters where one wrong step could have catastrophic consequences.

"Failure is a possibility, child," Maeve conceded, her voice devoid of false platitudes. "The path Kaelen has laid before you is fraught with peril. But so is the path of inaction. If you do nothing, if you try to bury this awakening, the Veil will not forget you. The forces you have stirred will continue to churn, and you may find yourself swept away by them regardless. Kaelen's offer of protection is not merely goodwill. It is practical necessity. He understands the dangers that now surround you, dangers that extend far beyond his own court."

Maeve's gaze drifted toward the window, reflecting distant concern. "The Fae are not a monolithic entity, Elara. There are courts, factions, ancient rivalries stretching back millennia. Kaelen, though he bears the mark of the Unseelie, is not necessarily aligned with all of them. His plight may attract the attention of those who would see his curse, and anyone connected to it, extinguished. His offer is an attempt to safeguard not only himself, but you as well. To ensure you are not inadvertently destroyed in the ensuing chaos."

A flicker of determination, small but persistent, began to burn within Elara. The same spark that ignited when a stubborn seedling refused to sprout, the same tenacity she applied when searching for rare herbs. The sheer impossibility of it all was overwhelming, yes, but it was also exhilarating. A terrifying, heart-pounding exhilaration. The Fae prince, with his sorrowful eyes and desperate plea, had planted a seed of purpose within her. To be considered capable, even if born of desperation, was to acknowledge a potential she had never dared dream of.

"So, I have to learn?" Elara asked, her voice gaining strength. "Learn about Fae curses, about the Veil, about whatever it is that binds him?"

The idea of delving into ancient lore, into hidden corners of magic, was both daunting and strangely compelling. A world away from the familiar scent of dried lavender and chamomile. A world of secrets and power.

"Precisely," Maeve affirmed, a hint of a smile touching her lips. "We must learn. The texts I possess, passed down through generations of my family, speak of the ancient balance between realms, of the ebb and flow of magical energies, and of the intricate workings of the Veil. They are not easy reading, child. They are filled with riddles, with allegorical language, and with warnings of profound risks. But they are our best starting point. Kaelen's knowledge is vast, I am sure, but it is colored by his own experiences, his own burdens. We must seek a broader understanding before we can truly hope to navigate this treacherous terrain."

Elara's gaze fell upon her own hands. Hands that had so often crushed herbs for poultices and tinctures. They looked so ordinary, so ill-equipped for the monumental task ahead. Yet Kaelen had seen something in them. Something beyond their mundane utility. He had seen the echo of the Veil, the resonance Maeve spoke of. Perhaps it was time to trust in that vision, even if she could not yet fully grasp its meaning.

"When do we begin?" she asked quietly.

The days that followed were a blur of activity unlike anything Elara had experienced. Maeve, despite her frail body, seemed to draw upon reserves of energy Elara hadn't known existed. The old woman retrieved dusty tomes from hidden corners of their cottage, books bound in cracked leather and written in languages that shifted and changed under Elara's gaze. Some passages glowed faintly in the lamplight, as if the words themselves held residual magic.

Elara learned of the Veil's creation, a collaborative effort between the mortal and Fae realms millennia ago. It had not been built to separate, but to protect. To regulate the flow of magic between worlds, to prevent either realm from overwhelming the other. But like any barrier, it required maintenance, a delicate balance of energies that had grown increasingly unstable over recent centuries.

The curse Kaelen spoke of was older than she had imagined. It did not simply afflict his bloodline. It was tied to the Veil itself, a parasitic force that fed on the boundary's instability and, in turn, weakened it further. A vicious cycle that threatened both realms.

"The curse seeks to unravel the Veil," Maeve explained one evening, her finger tracing ancient diagrams in one of the texts. "And in doing so, it feeds upon the magic of those most closely connected to its maintenance. The royal bloodlines of the Fae courts were the original architects, the keepers of the balance. They bear the deepest connection to the Veil, and thus they suffer most when it falters."

Elara absorbed this knowledge with growing understanding. Kaelen's desperation made more sense now. He wasn't simply trying to save his people from a personal affliction. He was trying to prevent the collapse of the very boundary that kept chaos at bay.

"But how can I help?" Elara asked. "What can I possibly do that the Fae themselves cannot?"

Maeve's eyes grew distant. "The Fae are powerful, child, but they are also bound by the limitations of their nature. They are creatures of magic, born from it, sustained by it. They cannot step outside its influence to see it objectively. You, however, possess something unique. You are mortal, yet you resonate with the Veil. You can bridge both worlds, see from both perspectives. This duality is what makes you vital. You can touch the Veil without being consumed by it. You can mend what they cannot."

The weight of responsibility settled heavier on Elara's shoulders with each passing day. But alongside the fear grew something else. Purpose. Direction. For the first time in her life, she felt she was working toward something that truly mattered.

Kaelen returned several nights later. This time, his arrival was quieter, less dramatic. He appeared at their threshold like a shadow coalescing from the darkness, his silver eyes finding Elara immediately.

"Have you made your decision?" he asked simply.

Elara met his gaze steadily. In the days since his first visit, she had wrestled with fear, doubt, and uncertainty. But she had also discovered a core of strength she hadn't known existed. The knowledge Maeve had shared, the understanding of what was at stake, had crystallized her resolve.

"I will help you," she said. "But I have conditions."

A flicker of surprise crossed Kaelen's face, followed by something that might have been respect. "Name them."

"I will not be a tool to be used and discarded," Elara stated firmly. "I will be a partner in this endeavor. You will teach me everything I need to know about the Fae, about your court, about the dangers I will face. You will not hide things from me to spare me fear or discomfort. I need the truth, all of it, if I am to be effective."

Kaelen studied her for a long moment, then inclined his head. "Agreed. What else?"

"My grandmother comes with us, or I do not go at all. Her knowledge is invaluable, and I will not leave her unprotected here. If your enemies know of me, they may seek to use her against me."

"Also agreed," Kaelen said without hesitation. "Maeve's wisdom will be welcome in my court. She will be treated with the respect due to one of her stature."

Elara took a deep breath. "And finally, if at any point I believe the path we are taking will cause more harm than good, you will listen to my concerns. You will not dismiss them simply because I am mortal and inexperienced. My connection to the Veil is what you seek. That means my instincts about it matter."

Kaelen's expression softened. "You have my word, Elara of Oakhaven. Your voice will be heard and valued. You are not a tool, but an ally. A partner, as you said."

He extended his hand toward her. "Then we have an accord?"

Elara looked at his outstretched hand, long-fingered and elegant, yet bearing the weight of centuries. She thought of her simple life in Oakhaven, of the quiet routines she would be leaving behind. She thought of the dangers ahead, the political machinations, the hostile court that awaited her. But she also thought of the Veil, of the humming resonance she felt deep in her bones, of the purpose that had awakened within her.

She placed her hand in his.

"We have an accord."

The nexus point where they would cross into the Faewild lay deeper in the woods than Elara had ever ventured. Kaelen led the way, with Elara and Maeve following close behind. Despite her age and illness, Maeve moved with surprising determination, her eyes bright with a mixture of fear and excitement that Elara recognized in herself.

The trees grew strange as they walked. Their bark took on an iridescent sheen, and their leaves whispered in languages Elara couldn't quite understand but felt she should recognize. The air grew thick with magic, tangible as fog.

"The boundary thins here," Kaelen explained, his voice low. "This is one of the oldest crossing points, used by my ancestors long before the courts divided into Seelie and Unseelie. It is neutral ground, protected by ancient accords."

They emerged into a clearing where the Veil was visible as a shimmering curtain of light. It rippled like water disturbed by an unfelt breeze, iridescent and beautiful. Elara felt its pull immediately, the resonance in her bones intensifying to an almost painful degree.

"It's magnificent," she breathed.

"And fragile," Kaelen added quietly. "More so than it should be. Can you feel the instability?"

Elara focused, reaching out with the sensitivity Maeve had helped her develop over the past days. Beneath the beauty, she could sense it. A trembling, like a string pulled too tight. Fractures running through the barrier, invisible to the eye but tangible to her inner sense.

"Yes," she whispered. "It's like glass about to shatter."

"That is the curse at work," Kaelen said grimly. "It feeds on the Veil's weakness, and in feeding, creates more weakness. A parasitic cycle that will eventually destroy both the barrier and those connected to it."

He turned to face her fully. "Once we cross, there is no turning back, Elara. Not immediately. The path to my court is long, and the journey itself is part of the trial. The Faewild tests all who enter it, mortal or Fae. It will show you wonders and horrors alike. You must be prepared."

Elara straightened her shoulders. "I am as prepared as I can be. The question is, are you prepared for what I might become in the process?"

A genuine smile crossed Kaelen's face, the first she had seen from him. "That, Elara of Oakhaven, is what I am counting on."

He offered his hand once more. This time, when she took it, she felt a surge of magic pass between them. A connection forging, a bond forming. Her own power, dormant for so long, rose to meet his, and the Veil responded. The shimmer intensified, the barrier thinning at that precise spot, creating a passage.

"Together," Kaelen said softly.

"Together," Elara echoed.

And with Maeve at her side, she stepped through the Veil and into the Faewild.

Chapter 3

The air thrummed with palpable anticipation as Kaelen's gaze met Elara's. The nexus, the tear in reality they had found, now pulsed with new intensity. No longer a fleeting shimmer of possibility, it had become a gateway deliberately forged. A permanent artery between their worlds.

Kaelen's hands moved with focused grace, tracing intricate patterns in the air. The emerald and sapphire hues of the Veil deepened, drew together, and formed a swirling vortex. A breathtaking spectacle of raw, untamed power. It was a maelstrom of light and energy, humming a low, resonant song that vibrated in Elara's bones.

"This is it, Elara," Kaelen said, his voice edged with reverence. "The true passage. Once crossed, there is no easy return."

Elara swallowed, her throat suddenly dry. She looked at the portal, a riot of impossible colors, then back at Kaelen. His silver eyes, usually filled with ancient knowledge and cool authority, now held a depth of emotion that resonated with her own. He wasn't simply leading her into danger. He was entrusting her with his world and his hope.

"I understand," she whispered, barely audible above the Veil's hum.

Kaelen's thumb brushed her knuckles in quiet reassurance. "When you step through, you enter a dream that has slumbered for millennia. The Faewild does not follow the laws of your world. Its beauty is as potent as its peril."

With a shared nod, Kaelen led her forward. The moment her boots touched the swirling light, she plunged into an ancient, vibrant tapestry woven from starlight and elemental magic. The air was thick with an unseen force that prickled her skin and whispered secrets at her ears. It carried scents alien yet strangely familiar, like memories she had never lived.

The landscape before her defied earthly comparison. Towering flora pulsed with inner luminescence. Petals unfurled in slow, deliberate movements. Leaves shimmered with iridescence, and an otherworldly glow painted everything in shades of amethyst, jade, and sapphire. The ground seemed to breathe, shifting with subtle life. Roots snaked like living veins, and moss carpeted the earth in glowing patterns. Luminescent fungi dotted the undergrowth, casting eerie, beautiful light that danced with deeper shadows.

Elara tightened her grip on Kaelen's hand, her breath catching. The alien beauty was intoxicating, a symphony of sights, scents, and sounds that flooded her mind. Every nerve tingled with energy. Gravity felt lighter, replaced by a buoyant sense that the atmosphere itself was welcoming her.

"It's incredible," she breathed, eyes wide as she tried to absorb the impossible panorama. The colors were deeper than anything she had known, the light softer yet more intense. Magic thrummed around her, a constant pulse that resonated with the nascent power within her.

Kaelen's grip tightened. "This is only the periphery. The true heart of the Faewild can awe and consume. Here, the veil between dreams and reality is thin. What you perceive and believe can manifest. Be mindful of your thoughts."

He guided her forward, their footsteps soft on the yielding ground. The glowing plants seemed to bend as they passed, either in greeting or warning. The air grew heavier, the scents more heady. A blend of unknown florals and earthy musk. Strange, melodic chirps and rustles echoed from the luminous foliage, hinting at unseen creatures.

"The flora is not merely beautiful. It is alive with magic," Kaelen murmured. He gestured to a cluster of flowers with petals like spun moonlight. "These blossoms absorb ambient magic and release it as light and fragrance. They mark the Veil's strength in this region."

Elara ran her hand through the air, feeling currents of energy flow around them. It was like swimming in a sea of pure potential. Exhilarating and disorienting. Her own magic stirred, answering the Faewild's call. It felt like coming home in a way Oakhaven never had.

As they ventured deeper, the land grew more fantastical. Trees with bark like polished obsidian twisted toward a twilight sky pricked with unfamiliar constellations. Thick vines beaded with glowing dew dripped nectar that shimmered with inner light. The air hummed with unspoken spells, ancient enchantments woven into the realm itself.

"My enemies will sense your presence," Kaelen said, scanning the terrain. "They are attuned to any disturbance in the Veil. Your crossing and your connection will draw them."

Elara's resolve held firm. She had come to help Kaelen and understand herself. Fear whispered at the edge of her thoughts, but no longer ruled her. "We knew this might happen. I'm not here to hide."

A faint smile touched his lips. "This path will be full of illusions and temptations meant to break your spirit. They will prey on your fears and doubts. Remember what we spoke of. Remember the truth of your power and the bond that links us."

He held her gaze. "The curse has scarred my people and the

Veil itself. Its decay has weakened the barriers, letting shadows creep in. My rivals want to harness that decay and the chaos it brings. Your ability to mend and reinforce the Veil threatens them."

They walked for what felt like hours, though time here flowed by the waxing and waning of ambient magic rather than the sun. Kaelen pointed out flora with unique properties and explained subtle shifts in air pressure that signaled magical flux.

"The farther we go from the nexus, the stronger the Unseelie Court's influence," he said. "Lord Valerius and Lady Seraphina are masters of manipulation with reach in every corner of this realm."

Elara absorbed his words, feeling the weight of his responsibility. Her latent abilities, once a curiosity, now felt like a vital defense against encroaching darkness.

"What do they ultimately want?" she asked. "Beyond seizing power."

"They want to control the Veil entirely," Kaelen replied, expression grim. "To twist its energies to their will and reshape the realms to their liking. In their vision, the balance that has kept chaos at bay would shatter. They believe in strength through domination, seeing compassion and cooperation as weakness."

He paused by a crystalline stream that sang as it flowed. "Lady Seraphina is perhaps the most dangerous. She is patient, methodical. Her plans span centuries. She cultivates alliances and enmities with equal care, always positioning herself to survive and thrive regardless of who sits on the throne. Her loyalty is only to herself and her vision of order through absolute control."

"And Lord Valerius?"

"More direct in his ambition," Kaelen said. "He believes in the old ways, when the Unseelie ruled through fear and power. He sees my efforts to break the curse as weakness, an attempt to deny our true nature. To him, the curse is a test, and my failure to embrace it marks me as unworthy."

As they walked, Elara noticed the landscape subtly changing. The ethereal beauty remained, but underlying menace grew more apparent. Shadows lingered longer. The music in the air took on discordant notes. Plants that had seemed welcoming now showed thorns and poisonous hues.

"We're entering territories they influence more directly," Kaelen explained. "The Faewild responds to the intent and power of those who inhabit it. Where Valerius holds sway, the land reflects his nature. Dark. Predatory."

They passed groves where the trees whispered not in welcome but in warning. Elara heard snatches of words in languages she didn't know but somehow understood. Threats. Challenges. Claims of dominion.

"Don't listen to them," Kaelen said firmly. "They're testing you, trying to find weaknesses in your resolve. The Faewild is alive, and it judges all who enter. Show no fear."

Elara straightened her shoulders, meeting the whispers with silence and determination. Gradually, the hostile murmurs faded, as if the land itself recognized her strength.

They paused beside a waterfall of liquid moonlight, and Kaelen turned to face her fully. His expression was shadowed, the usual mask of princely composure slipping.

"The curse that binds me is one burden among many," he said quietly. "The Unseelie Court is a viper's nest. Ambition is the currency, and loyalty a passing shadow. My claim to the throne draws constant contention."

He chose his words with care. "My father is formidable. His reign has been long, and his grip is no longer absolute. That space invites ambition."

Elara waited, sensing he needed to unburden himself of truths he rarely spoke aloud.

"Many think themselves better suited to rule," Kaelen went on, bitterness edging his tone. "Among them, my own blood runs coldest. My younger brother, Malakor. Charismatic, with a silver tongue and influence wielded with ruthless precision."

Elara's breath hitched. "He undermines you?"

"Undermines is gentle," Kaelen said with a humorless laugh. "He sabotages my efforts, sows discord, and paints me as weak or indecisive. He sees my curse as an opportunity to claim the throne and recast our court in an image darker and more brutal than it is now."

He rubbed his brow, suddenly looking tired despite his immortal nature. "His ambition is bottomless. He's gathered like-minded lords who chafe under my father's rule. Even their loyalty to him is transactional."

"And Lady Seraphina?" Elara prompted, remembering the name.

"She is different," Kaelen said, voice lower. "Ancient lineage tied to the oldest magical currents. She has advised my father for centuries. Her intellect is keen, her arcane knowledge deep, and her plans stretch for decades. Her loyalty is to herself. She anticipates shifts in power and positions herself to benefit no matter who rules."

He looked into the falling moonlight. "Malakor grabs power through force and deception. Seraphina shapes the flow of power so she remains indispensable. Their presence creates constant pressure. Vigilance must reach beyond the physical to intent and ambition."

The truth of Kaelen's life settled on Elara. She had come to understand his curse, but now she saw another curse. The weight of legacy and the politics that circled him like wolves.

"It sounds exhausting," Elara said softly.

"It is a war on many fronts," he answered. "My father is powerful but increasingly detached, leaving daily dealings to me. And I am compromised." He gestured to himself. "My affliction makes me a target. Doubt follows my every action."

Elara stepped closer. "You are strong, Kaelen. Strategic. You must have allies."

A genuine smile touched his mouth. "I do. Those who want a just and stable court. But they are fewer than those swayed by Malakor or weary of my father's reign. Even allies risk their positions by standing with me."

The glade where they rested held rare quiet. Ferns unfurled like emerald lace, and the air hummed with soft magic. Here, Kaelen's armor of control showed small cracks.

Elara noticed a jagged scrape on his forearm, a token of the Faewild's wildness. She knelt beside him and cleaned it gently, her fingers trembling with empathy.

"This terrain is more unforgiving than I expected," she murmured.

Kaelen watched her, his guarded expression easing. Gratitude flickered in his eyes. "The Faewild guards its secrets. It does not suffer intrusion, even for a prince."

He motioned to the bioluminescent foliage. "This is my kingdom, yet I am a stranger on some paths. The curse clouds more than blood. It dims my connection to the land I should protect."

Elara wrapped his forearm with clean linen, her touch lingering. "It must be lonely."

"Lonely," he echoed. "Yes. One learns distance. To observe rather than join. Every smile, every word must be weighed for motive. Trust is a luxury."

His gaze drifted beyond the glade. "Even in my father's halls, I am ringed by those who would exploit weakness. To inherit power and responsibility while those closest threaten it is a bitter thing."

Elara's hand covered his. A simple gesture of solidarity that spoke volumes. "You're not alone anymore," she said quietly. "Whatever lies ahead, we face it together."

For a moment, Kaelen's careful mask crumbled entirely. Raw emotion crossed his face, gratitude and relief and something deeper. Something neither of them was quite ready to name.

"Together," he repeated, his voice rough with feeling. "Yes."

The moment stretched between them, fragile and profound. Then Kaelen gently squeezed her hand and rose to his feet, the princely composure sliding back into place like well-worn armor.

"We should continue," he said. "The court awaits, and there is much you need to see before we arrive."

But as they walked on through the luminous forest, their hands remained clasped. And the Faewild around them seemed to sing a little brighter, as if even the land itself recognized the bond forming between them.

Chapter 4

The approach to the Unseelie Court was an experience that defied mortal comprehension. As Kaelen led Elara deeper into the heart of the Faewild, the landscape transformed from ethereal beauty into something far more deliberate. More controlled. The wild magic that had surrounded them in the outer realms gave way to power shaped by will and intention.

They descended into a vast chasm, a geographic wound in the land itself. The walls were sheer obsidian, polished to a mirror-like finish that reflected not just light but something deeper. Something older. Elara caught glimpses of her own reflection, but also fleeting images of things that had never been. Shadows of possible futures or echoes of forgotten pasts.

Above them, the sky was no longer the twilight expanse of the outer Faewild. Here, captured stars burned in a firmament of eternal night. Each star was a prisoner, Kaelen explained quietly, bound by ancient magic to illuminate the Court below. The effect was both magnificent and unsettling. Beautiful yet wrong in a fundamental way.

"They were willing sacrifices," Kaelen said when he saw her troubled expression. "Stars that chose to illuminate the Court rather than burn alone in the void. Or so the stories claim. Truth and legend blur here."

The ground thrummed with restless energy, resonating through Elara's bones. This was not the wild, untamed magic of the outer realms. It was concentrated. Deliberate. Power honed by generations of ruthless will. The air felt charged, thick with unspoken currents of ancient alliances, bitter rivalries, and the constant hum of magic woven and unwoven in intricate patterns.

As they descended a winding path carved into the obsidian cliff face, the true scale of the Court revealed itself. Flora unlike anything Elara had seen bloomed in the perpetual twilight. Flowers with iridescent petals pulsed with inner light, their stems like spun glass. Delicate and sharp. Vines bore dark, jewel-toned fruits that absorbed starlight, their leaves edged in silver luminescence. The beauty was undeniable, but it was sharp-edged and dangerous. Nature twisted and molded by unforgiving will.

The entrance was not a gate but a vast maw in the obsidian that seemed to swallow light whole. As they stepped through, the wind died, and the oppressive silence of the precipice yielded to a low, resonant murmur. The sound of thousands of presences. Not speaking so much as existing. A collective awareness that washed over Elara like a tide.

Then she saw them. The courtiers.

They moved through grand halls, appearing and disappearing in the interplay of light and shadow. Beings of impossible beauty and chilling demeanor. Some were tall and lithe, their movements fluid as serpents, their skin the color of polished ivory or midnight blue. Others were smaller, more ephemeral, their wings blurs of iridescent gossamer. Their garments were works of art. Flowing silks woven from moonlight and shadow, adorned with jewels that pulsed with cold inner fire.

It was their eyes that unsettled Elara most. Ancient predators' eyes, sharp and assessing, yet impossibly beautiful. Some were chips of glacial ice, reflecting the captured starlight with unnerving clarity. Others burned like embers from a dying pyre, hinting at hidden passions and dangerous intensity. In all of them, she saw profound, ageless detachment. A chilling lack of warmth that spoke of a world far removed from mortal concerns.

Elara felt profoundly out of place. A fragile mortal, a creature of fleeting seasons and warmth, drifting in a sea of ancient, dangerous magic. The air felt thinner here, harder to draw into her lungs, as if it were not meant for her kind. Every rustle of silk, every whisper underscored her otherness. She clutched Kaelen's arm, knuckles white, taking subtle reassurance from his presence.

"They are magnificent," she whispered, the word inadequate.

Kaelen's grip tightened on her arm in silent acknowledgment. "Magnificence is often born from shadow, Elara. And power, in this realm, is rarely gentle."

He led her through a vast hall whose walls bore tapestries woven from moonlight and starlight. Scenes of ancient battles and forgotten triumphs shifting in their threads. The floor was a mosaic of obsidian and pearl, reflecting the cold light like a frozen lake. Courtiers paused, turning their impossibly beautiful faces toward them. Their gazes pricked at Elara like a thousand needles, dissecting her, assessing her worth or lack of it.

"This is my home, of sorts," Kaelen said, tone carefully neutral. "The heart of the Unseelie. Alliances are forged and broken here. Whispers carry more weight than shouts, and a single misstep can lead to lasting consequences."

He gestured to the ebb and flow around them. "Each carries a history and ambition. They are loyal to the crown, yes, but their loyalty is a currency to be spent or hoarded. They have seen empires rise and fall and ages turn. Their perspective is different from yours. Mortal lives pass in a blink."

Elara forced herself to meet the eyes that sought her, offering a small, hesitant smile. Most returned her gaze with unnerving impassivity. A few showed a flicker of curiosity or amusement. One Fae, a woman of ethereal beauty with hair like spun moonlight and emerald-chip eyes, gave Elara a slow, appraising look and a smile that did not reach her eyes. It promised danger.

"Do they know why I am here?" Elara asked, barely above a whisper.

Kaelen's silver eyes met hers, sympathy flickering in their depths. "Rumor is the lifeblood of any court, especially one steeped in intrigue. They know you are mortal and that you are with me. The specifics are left to speculation. Some think you a petitioner seeking a boon. Others, a prisoner, though you do not look the part. And some whisper of prophecy, of a mortal hand destined to intervene." He paused. "For now, you are the mortal who accompanies the Prince. That alone invites debate."

They moved deeper into the Court. The captured stars burned brighter here, their cold fire illuminating chambers filled with treasures that took Elara's breath. Chests overflowing with gems that pulsed with inner light. Weapons forged from unknown metals. Tapestries woven with threads of pure magic. Yet among the wealth was restraint. A dark beauty that hinted at something withheld and dangerous.

"The Unseelie Court is not merely a place of power," Kaelen said, his voice resonant. "It reflects what we are. Beings of balance. Shadow and light. Creation and destruction. Our beauty is often forged in darkness, our strength tempered by sorrow. Here, the natural order is understood. Predator and prey move in a delicate, eternal dance."

He stopped and faced her. Courtiers gave them a wider berth, forming a circle of respectful distance. "Honesty is rare here. Words are veiled. Intentions hide beneath courtesy. Trust is earned slowly. The greatest danger comes not from open hostility but from silken whispers that wrap around your throat before you realize you're choking."

He brushed his fingers against her cheek, both tender and possessive. "You are a beacon of sincerity in a realm that shuns it. That is your strength and your vulnerability. Be wary. Observe. Listen. Above all, do not let this darkness extinguish the light you carry."

Elara leaned into his touch, comfort and unease swirling within. Kaelen was her anchor in this alien landscape, yet the sheer weight of the Court pressed down on her. This was a place of ancient power, breathtaking beauty, and danger so profound it seeped from the stones themselves.

The first days in the Court passed in a bewildering blur. Elara found herself constantly off-balance, navigating a world where every interaction carried hidden weight and meaning. Kaelen had arranged quarters for her in a tower overlooking the chasm, rooms that were beautiful in their stark elegance but felt more like a gilded cage than a sanctuary.

She saw little of Kaelen those first days. He was consumed with court business, meetings with his father and advisors, negotiations with various factions. When they did cross paths, he was always surrounded by courtiers, his princely mask firmly in place. The vulnerability she'd glimpsed during their journey seemed to have evaporated in the cold light of the Court.

It was during these lonely hours that she first encountered Malakor.

Kaelen's younger brother appeared in her doorway on the third evening of her stay, announced only by the sudden chill in the air. He was beautiful in the way all Fae were beautiful, but where Kaelen's beauty was severe and restrained, Malakor's was indulgent. Sensual. His dark hair fell in artful disarray, and his eyes held warmth that somehow felt more dangerous than Kaelen's cool silver.

"The mysterious mortal," he said, voice smooth as honey over steel. "Forgive the intrusion. I could not resist meeting the woman who has so thoroughly captured my brother's attention."

Elara rose from the window seat where she'd been attempting to read one of the texts Maeve had provided. "Prince Malakor. I've heard much about you."

"All terrible, I'm sure," he said with a disarming smile. "Kaelen does enjoy painting me as the villain in his tragic tale. May I?" He gestured to the room.

Something in Elara warned against allowing him entry, but refusing seemed equally dangerous. "Of course."

Malakor moved through her quarters with the ease of someone who knew them well, trailing his fingers along surfaces, examining the few personal items she'd brought. "You must find it terribly dull, being locked away up here. Kaelen always was overly cautious. Protective to the point of suffocation."

"He's been very kind," Elara said carefully.

"Kind." Malakor laughed, the sound genuinely amused. "Yes, Kaelen excels at kindness. Duty. Honor. All the virtues that make for an excellent prince and a terribly boring companion." He turned to face her fully. "Tell me, Elara of Oakhaven. What did my brother promise you? Power? Protection? The breaking of an ancient curse?"

His tone made it clear he knew exactly why she was here.

"He asked for my help," Elara said. "I chose to give it."

"Chose." Malakor savored the word. "How refreshing. Most mortals who cross the Veil have that choice made for them. You must be special indeed." He moved closer, and Elara fought the urge to step back. "Or perhaps foolish. Has Kaelen told you the true cost of breaking a curse that has plagued our bloodline for generations? Has he explained that such magic requires sacrifice? That healing one wound often opens another?"

"He has been honest with me about the dangers."

"Honest." Another word Malakor seemed to find amusing. "My brother has a talent for selective honesty. He tells you enough to secure your cooperation while withholding the truths that might send you fleeing back through the Veil." He tilted his head, studying her. "The Solstice approaches. Three weeks from now, the realms will align, and the Veil will be at its thinnest. It is the only time when such a curse might be broken. But it is also when the Court is at its most dangerous. When power shifts and alliances are tested."

Three weeks. The timeline settled in Elara's mind like a weight. Three weeks to prepare, to learn, to somehow become strong enough to face whatever was coming.

"Kaelen seeks to use the Solstice to break his curse," Malakor continued. "But others have their own plans for that night. Plans that may not align with my brother's noble intentions." He reached into his robes and withdrew a small box made of dark wood. "A gift. Whisperwood, carved by artisans who have long since passed into legend. It has certain properties. The ability to capture and hold secrets. Whispers. The unspoken truths that fill this court like poison gas."

He offered it to her. "Keep it close. When you wish to know what is truly being said about you, about Kaelen, about anything at all, simply open it in a quiet place and listen. The box remembers."

Elara stared at the box but did not take it. "Why would you give me this?"

"Because," Malakor said, smile sharpening, "you are a variable in a very delicate equation. Kaelen has placed great faith in you. Perhaps too much faith. I would hate to see you used and discarded when your purpose is served. The box gives you power. The power to know. To choose your own path rather than following blindly where my dutiful brother leads."

He set the box on the table between them. "I make no demands. No bargains. Simply an offer of knowledge. A tool that might help you survive what is coming." He moved toward the door, then paused. "The Solstice approaches, Elara. Choose your allegiances carefully. Not everyone who offers protection truly has your interests at heart. And not everyone painted as a villain is truly your enemy."

With that, he was gone, leaving behind only the chill in the air and the dark box sitting on her table like a coiled snake.

Elara stared at it for a long moment. Then, with trembling hands, she opened it. For now, it held only silence. But she knew that would change. In three weeks, at the Solstice, everything would change.

Chapter 5

The weight of Kaelen's unspoken words settled between them, a tangible presence in the quiet library. Elara felt a tremor run through her, a mix of apprehension and thrilling, dangerous hope. The prince's admission, his vulnerability, had chipped away at the formidable façade he usually presented. He saw her. Truly saw her. And in his gaze, she found a reflection of a strength she hadn't realized she possessed.

Yet the Unseelie Court was a treacherous landscape, and her place within it, as a mortal, was precarious. Her attraction to Kaelen was a dangerous spark in a tinderbox of political intrigue and ancient curses. She had to be cautious and remember the chasm that separated their worlds, the inherent dangers that clung to him like a regal cloak.

"I appreciate your honesty, Your Highness," she managed, her voice a little breathy as she consciously pulled back from the precipice of their shared gaze. "But there are many things I do not understand about this court, about your family. My resilience, as you call it, is born of necessity, not understanding."

Kaelen's jaw tightened almost imperceptibly. He stepped back, the subtle shift creating a space between them that Elara felt keenly. The moment of raw intimacy passed, replaced by the familiar formality of their roles. "Nevertheless," he said, his voice regaining some of its princely cadence, though an underlying warmth remained, "your perspective is valuable. And there are other matters concerning the heart of this court that I believe you are uniquely positioned to understand. Matters intrinsically linked to the affliction that plagues my lineage."

He turned, his silhouette stark against the glowing orbs that illuminated the library. "There is a place," he began, tone more somber, "a chamber deep within the ancient heart of the palace, rarely spoken of even among the highest echelons of my court. It is steeped in sorrow, and it is said to be the nexus of the curse that binds my family."

Elara's blood ran cold. She had heard whispers. Fragmented tales shared in hushed tones by servants and courtiers of a malediction that had afflicted Kaelen's ancestors for generations. A curse spoken of with fear and morbid fascination, a shadow that loomed over the Unseelie throne.

"The curse?" she breathed, the word barely audible.

Kaelen nodded, expression grave. "Indeed. It is not merely a spiritual ailment, Elara, but something more tangible, more insidious. It manifests as a gradual decay. A sapping of vitality, a creeping madness that has claimed many of my bloodline. My father, and his father before him, all succumbed to its slow embrace. I have studied the ancient texts, delving into the history of my house, searching for an answer, a cure, a way to break free from this inherited doom. And all paths, every prophecy and piece of forgotten lore, point to this chamber."

He extended a hand toward her, not in invitation but as if offering a shared burden. "The texts describe it as a place where the Veil between worlds is thinnest, where the raw energy of creation has been twisted and corrupted. It is where the ancestral pact, the one that granted my family power, was forged. And where it was broken."

Elara's mind raced. The Veil. The fragile barrier between

their worlds. Kaelen had spoken of its importance before, but this was different. This was personal. "You want me to go there with you," she said quietly. It wasn't a question.

"I do," he confirmed. "Your connection to the Veil is unlike anything I have encountered. You touched it during our crossing and emerged unscathed. More than that, you resonated with it. The ancient texts speak of those rare mortals who possess an affinity for the liminal spaces, who can bridge worlds without being consumed. I believe you are one such mortal, Elara. And I believe that together, we might uncover what my ancestors could not. The key to breaking this curse."

The weight of his expectation settled on her shoulders. Yet alongside the fear was something else. Purpose. A sense that this moment had been building since she first glimpsed him through the tear in the Veil.

"When?" she asked.

A flicker of relief crossed his features. "Tomorrow. After the court retires. The chamber is warded, accessible only to those of my bloodline. But with you at my side, with your connection to the Veil, we may be able to bypass some of those protections. To see what has been hidden for generations."

The next evening came too quickly. Elara spent the day in nervous anticipation, her mind churning with possibilities and fears. What if she wasn't strong enough? What if her connection to the Veil wasn't what Kaelen believed it to be? What if they failed?

When the summons came, delivered by a silent servant, her hands trembled as she dressed. She chose simple clothing, practical rather than ornamental. Whatever they faced in that chamber, she suspected courtly finery would be of little use.

Kaelen met her in a shadowed corridor far from the main

halls. He wore dark leathers rather than his usual princely robes, practical garb that spoke of the seriousness of their undertaking. His expression was grave but determined.

"Are you certain?" he asked, giving her one last opportunity to withdraw.

Elara straightened her shoulders. "I am."

They descended. Down past the familiar levels of the palace, into regions Elara had never seen. The air grew colder, the stone older. Ancient magic thrummed through the walls, making her skin prickle with awareness. The deeper they went, the more oppressive the atmosphere became.

Finally, they reached a door. Not the ornate, beautiful portals that marked the rest of the palace, but something crude. Ancient. Carved from a single slab of dark stone and covered in symbols that seemed to writhe in the dim light.

Kaelen placed his palm against it. The symbols flared with cold light, and Elara felt a pulse of magic sweep over them both. Testing. Judging. For a moment, she thought the door would reject them. Then, with a grinding sound that spoke of centuries of disuse, it swung open.

The chamber beyond stole her breath.

It was vast, far larger than should have been possible given their depth beneath the palace. The ceiling was lost in shadow, and the walls seemed to pulse with a sickly, organic rhythm. At the center of the chamber sat a basin carved from obsidian, filled with a liquid so dark it seemed to absorb light rather than reflect it.

"The heart of the curse," Kaelen said quietly, his voice echoing strangely in the cavernous space. "This is where it began."

Elara moved closer, drawn despite her fear. The liquid in the basin pulsed in time with her heartbeat, as if sensing her presence. "What is it?"

"Corrupted essence," Kaelen replied, following her. "When my ancestor broke the pact with the Veil, this is what remained. The exchange that once flowed freely between realms became stagnant. Poisoned. And it has been feeding on my bloodline ever since."

He gestured to tapestries hanging on the walls. Elara hadn't noticed them at first, but now she saw they depicted a history. The forging of the pact. The power it granted. And then, in stark imagery, the breaking. The consequences.

"My father believed this chamber was a wound to be sealed," Kaelen said, his knuckles white as he gripped the edge of the basin. "He never understood the curse wasn't contained here. The chamber manifests its hunger. It needs to feed."

"We're standing in its feeding ground," Elara said quietly, understanding dawning. "But if it feeds on life force, perhaps it can be satiated or redirected. The original pact was an exchange. What if the solution is to re-establish that exchange? To restore the flow?"

She gestured to the tapestries. "They record depletion. Passive draining. What if we introduce an active, reciprocal exchange? Something sustainable?"

Kaelen's eyes widened. "An active exchange. The pact's dissolution turned circulation into hemorrhage." He looked at the basin with renewed focus. "The texts speak of the 'Blood of the First Pact.' My father saw appeasement. But what if it was reconnection? 'Blood' as vital essence. 'Pact' as the ritual ensuring a balanced flow."

"If the Veil consumes to restore itself," he continued,

voice gaining strength, "perhaps the answer is not to fight it, but to offer a sustainable source of nourishment. To complete the circuit."

A fragile stillness fell. The pulse of the dark liquid slowed, as if listening.

Elara and Kaelen shared an understanding. They had found not only the source, but a path to its undoing. The question was how.

"The Veil is a tapestry," Kaelen said. "This chamber is a wound where the threads unravel. We must touch those threads to understand the tear." He gestured to the basin. "The ritual requires a direct connection. Your touch will be the conduit. Seek the flow."

Elara breathed in the humid air. The despair felt less like a shroud now and more like a turbulent sea hiding truths beneath its surface. She extended her hand, fingers trembling not with fear but with awareness. This was a magic she had always felt, earth-tethered and primal, but had never named.

Warmth radiated from the liquid like a feverish brow. Kaelen's steady presence anchored her. She recalled the Veil's luminous weave during their crossing and reached not with her hand but with her will. Dipping into cool current rather than viscous mire. She found a whisper of the original pact, a hum of harmonious exchange.

Her fingertips touched the surface.

The liquid surged upward. Not splashing but coiling. A viscous tendril wrapped her fingers. It was icy and pulsed with parasitic hunger. Elara gasped as a sliver of vitality leached away.

"Hold on," Kaelen urged, close and urgent. "Do not pull

away. Feel its hunger, but do not yield."

Yielding had birthed the curse. Elara steadied herself, focusing on starlight and earth-pulse. She willed her energy to become resilient like a well-rooted tree in a storm.

The tendril tightened, cold seeping deeper. Panic pressed in. The curse sought to drain her completely.

"The ritual isn't resistance," Kaelen murmured. "It is redirection. Your touch reminds it how to connect. Offer a different nourishment."

Elara understood. If it craved life force, she would offer a vibrant, balanced pulse. The scent of rain. Sunlight on skin. The quiet resilience of a seed. Pure, uncorrupted essence.

The tendril recoiled slightly. The cold softened to a questioning warmth, as if bewildered by the offering. The liquid's pulse slowed. Elara pictured vibrant strands of the Veil and wove her energy into them. Not to force a mend, but as gentle reinforcement. A reminder.

The curse fought back. Heat seared with concentrated despair. Elara cried out as her focus frayed. Weakness crept in.

"No, Elara!" Kaelen's hand found her shoulder, firm and grounding. "You are not fighting it. You are understanding it. Show it another way."

She drew strength from his touch and their shared purpose. She was not a sacrifice, but a participant. She guided her energy like water cooling a fire. Porous, allowing contact without surrender.

The heat subsided. The tendril hesitated, aggression softening into yearning. A wound craving healing. Elara wove again: stars in a night sky, mountains' quiet strength, a brook's exuberance. An invitation, not an imposition.

The liquid swirled, its blackness softening with iridescence. The tendril loosened and withdrew, leaving her hand cool but intact. The basin still pulsed, slower now. Contemplative.

"It's not about destroying the curse," Elara said, voice steady despite her exhaustion. "It's about re-establishing balance. The curse is the Veil's distorted hunger. By offering a different nourishment, a reminder of the pact, we coax it toward equilibrium."

She flexed her tingling fingers. Tired, but unbroken.

"The 'Blood of the First Pact,'" Kaelen mused. "Not appeasement. Vital essence. Your offering was life itself."

He turned to her, eyes bright with hope and conviction. "You have touched the Veil and offered solace. Not a solution yet, but a beginning. The curse can be soothed. The Veil can be reminded."

Elara held his gaze, fragile strength blooming within her. The chamber was still a wound, but not only a place of despair. She had touched the curse's heart and glimpsed the possibility of healing. The Veil was not an enemy, but a wounded entity seeking understanding. In that understanding, and in their shared purpose, lay a glimmer of hope.

But the peace shattered.

The basin erupted without warning. The dark liquid didn't splash—it exploded upward in a column of writhing shadow and sickly emerald light. The curse, sensing their understanding, their attempt to heal it, reacted with primal fury.

"Elara, back!" Kaelen shouted, pulling her away from the basin.

Too late. The darkness coalesced into form, a spectral entity, neither solid nor shadow, but something in between. Ancient and malevolent, it radiated hunger and rage in waves that pressed against Elara's mind like physical blows. This was the curse made manifest, the concentrated corruption of centuries given terrible shape.

The entity shrieked, a sound that existed more in the mind than the air, and lashed out with tendrils of emerald energy. Kaelen raised his hand, silver light flaring as he tried to shield them both, but the curse was too strong, too focused.

One tendril slipped past his defenses and struck him square in the side. The emerald beam seared through clothing and flesh alike. Kaelen cried out and dropped to one knee, his protective magic flickering and dying.

"No!" Elara grabbed his arm, pulling him toward the passage. The entity advanced, growing larger, feeding on their fear. The scent of ozone and ancient grief filled the chamber until breathing hurt.

Kaelen's hand found hers, gripping tight. "Run," he gasped. "Now."

They ran. Through the winding passages of the chamber, the entity's presence pursuing them like a suffocating tide. Elara could hear it behind them, or feel it, a psychic pressure that made her knees weak and her breath come in gasps. The starlight power within her felt small and fragile against such concentrated malevolence.

Suddenly and without explanation the entity dissipated into a thousand fractured elements.

Chapter 6

The silence after the spectral entity's dissipation was not peaceful. It was a heavy, suffocating blanket woven from the remnants of terror and stark realization. Elara's knees still felt weak. Her breath came in shallow gasps as she stared at the space where the curse had manifested. The air held the scent of ozone and something like ancient, bitter grief.

The encounter had been more than a physical trial. It was a psychic assault on her very being. The vibrant hum of starlight within her, so potent moments before, now felt like a fragile ember threatened by the immensity of what she had witnessed.

Her gaze drifted to Kaelen, who was still struggling to regain his footing, hand pressed to his side where the emerald beam had struck. The pallor of his skin and the pain etched into his features amplified the fear coiling in her stomach. She had always known the curse was a threat, but seeing its manifestation, feeling its hunger and destructive intent, chilled her to the bone.

"We need to leave," Kaelen said hoarsely, straightening with visible effort. "This chamber is not safe. The entity may return, and I am not certain I can withstand another assault."

Elara nodded, helping him steady himself. Together they made their way back through the winding passages, each step an effort. The ascent felt longer than the descent, every shadow seeming to hold potential danger.

By the time they reached Kaelen's chambers, exhaustion had set in fully. Elara helped him to a chair, then moved to fetch water and bandages for the wound at his side. The emerald energy had left a burn, angry and blistered.

"Let me see," she said softly.

Kaelen pulled aside his torn shirt, revealing the damage. The burn was worse than she'd feared, the edges blackened as if touched by corruption. She cleaned it gently, drawing on her herbalist training, and applied a poultice made from moonpetal and silverleaf.

"It will scar," she said quietly.

"All battles leave scars," Kaelen replied, voice distant. "Some visible, some not."

They sat in silence for a long moment, the weight of what they'd faced settling over them like snow. Finally, Kaelen spoke again.

"Eleven days," he said. "Eleven days until the Solstice. We have so little time, Elara. And now we know the curse can manifest physically. It can attack. All my research suggested it was merely a wasting disease, something that drained vitality slowly over generations. But this..." He gestured to his wound. "This is warfare."

Elara's mind raced. Eleven days. Less than two weeks to find a way to break a curse that had plagued his bloodline for centuries. Less than two weeks to prepare for whatever the Solstice would bring.

"We have more knowledge than we did before," she offered. "We know the curse has a consciousness. We know it can be weakened by hope, by starlight. That's something."

"Is it enough?" Kaelen asked, silver eyes meeting hers. For the first time since she'd known him, she saw true fear there. Not for himself, but for his people. For the realm. For her.

"It has to be," Elara said firmly. "We'll make it enough."

The days that followed were a blur of research and preparation. Kaelen threw himself into ancient texts with renewed urgency, barely sleeping, barely eating. Elara found herself pushed to the edges of his focus, a tool to be consulted when needed but otherwise kept at arm's length.

She understood. The pressure on him was immense. But understanding didn't make the distance hurt less.

It was during one of these lonely afternoons, wandering the palace gardens in search of fresh air and clarity, that Elara encountered Seraphina again.

The sorceress appeared as if from nowhere, materializing out of the jasmine-scented mist that perpetually shrouded this corner of the gardens. Her golden eyes fixed on Elara with unsettling intensity.

"You look troubled, child," Seraphina observed, her voice like rustling silk.

"I'm fine," Elara said automatically, then reconsidered. Seraphina was ancient, powerful, and had knowledge Elara desperately needed. "Actually, no. I'm not fine. The Solstice approaches, and I feel... unprepared. Like whatever power I have isn't enough."

Seraphina's lips curved in a knowing smile. "Ah. The eternal lament of those touched by greatness. The power you possess, Elara, is merely the seed. It must be cultivated, nurtured, and properly trained if it is to bloom."

She gestured to a nearby bench, and they sat. The sorceress produced a small leather-bound book from within her robes, its cover embossed with symbols that seemed to shift in the light.

"This is a primer," Seraphina said, "on celestial magic. The art of drawing power not from the earth or the Veil directly, but from the stars themselves. You have an affinity for starlight. It recognized you in that cursed chamber. But affinity alone is not mastery."

Elara took the book carefully, feeling warmth emanate from its pages. "Why help me? What do you gain from this?"

Seraphina's smile widened. "Direct. I appreciate that. What do I gain? Stability. Balance. Kaelen is... well-intentioned but limited in his understanding of true power. You, however, have potential. Potential that, if properly directed, could tip the scales in favor of order rather than chaos."

She leaned closer, voice dropping to a conspiratorial whisper. "The curse that afflicts his bloodline is but one threat among many. Malakor schemes. The Seelie Court watches. Ancient powers stir in the depths. If you wish to protect Kaelen, to truly be his partner rather than his burden, you must become powerful enough to stand beside him as an equal."

The words struck deep. Elara had felt the growing distance between herself and Kaelen, the sense that she was becoming more liability than asset. The thought of changing that, of becoming strong enough to truly help, was intoxicating.

"What would I need to do?" she asked.

"Study," Seraphina replied simply. "Practice. The book contains exercises, meditations, rituals. Some require sacrifice. Small things at first. A cherished memory. A lingering attachment to your old life. By releasing these anchors, you make space for celestial power to flow through you."

Something in Elara's chest tightened. "Sacrifice my memories?"

"Only the ones that hold you back," Seraphina said smoothly. "The ones that keep you tethered to who you were rather than who you must become. Think of it as shedding old skin. Necessary for growth."

Elara looked down at the book in her hands. The offer was tempting. But something about Seraphina's smile, about the way her eyes gleamed with hidden calculation, set off warning bells.

"I'll consider it," Elara said carefully, not committing.

"Do not consider too long," Seraphina warned. "Time grows short. Eleven days, as Prince Kaelen so aptly noted. Eleven days to become what you must be, or risk losing everything."

With that, the sorceress rose and glided away, leaving Elara alone with the book and her churning thoughts.

That evening, Elara tried to speak with Kaelen about her encounter with Seraphina. She found him in his study, surrounded by parchments and looking more haggard than she'd ever seen him.

"Kaelen," she said softly from the doorway.

He looked up, and for a moment his expression softened. Then duty reasserted itself. "Elara. Is something wrong?"

"I spoke with Lady Seraphina today. She offered to teach me celestial magic. To help me grow stronger before the Solstice."

Kaelen's jaw tightened almost imperceptibly. "Did she? How generous of her."

The sarcasm in his tone was unlike him. Elara stepped fully into the room. "You don't trust her."

"I don't trust anyone who offers power freely," Kaelen replied, turning back to his scrolls. "Seraphina serves her own interests. Always has. If she's offering to teach you, it's because she sees some advantage in it for herself."

"But what if I need that training?" Elara pressed. "What if the power I have now isn't enough to help you break the curse? Shouldn't I take whatever help I can get?"

Kaelen set down his quill with more force than necessary. "And what did she ask in return? What does this training require?"

Elara hesitated. "Sacrifice. Memories, attachments. She says they're anchors that limit my potential."

"Of course she did." Kaelen stood, moving to the window to stare out at the twilight sky. "That's how it begins, Elara. Small sacrifices. Then larger ones. Until you've given away so much of yourself that you no longer recognize who you've become."

He turned to face her, silver eyes intense. "I don't want that for you. I don't want you to lose yourself in pursuit of power. Your humanity, your memories, your attachments, those are what make you strong. Not liabilities to be shed."

"But I'm not strong enough," Elara said, frustration bleeding into her voice. "Not to help you. Not to stand beside you. I'm just the mortal girl who happened to have an affinity for the Veil. Against the curse, against Malakor, against everything this court throws at us, I'm..."

"You're everything," Kaelen interrupted, crossing the room to take her hands. "You're everything I never knew I needed. Your strength doesn't come from celestial magic or sacrificed memories. It comes from your heart. From your compassion. From the light you carry that has nothing to do with power and everything to do with who you are."

His grip tightened. "Please, Elara. Don't let Seraphina or anyone else convince you that you need to become something else. Something more. You're already enough."

For a moment, the distance between them vanished. Elara saw past the tired prince to the man beneath. The one who had confided in her, laughed with her, trusted her.

But then the moment passed. Kaelen released her hands and stepped back, the walls reasserting themselves.

"I have to return to my research," he said, voice formal once more. "The council meets tomorrow to discuss the Solstice preparations. I need to have answers."

"Of course," Elara said quietly, the familiar hurt settling back over her heart. "I'll leave you to it."

She made it to the door before Kaelen spoke again.

"Elara."

She turned.

"Be careful with Seraphina. She collects people the way others collect jewels. I would hate to see you become another treasure in her hoard."

Elara nodded and left, the warning echoing in her mind.

That night, alone in her chambers, Elara opened Seraphina's book. The pages were filled with intricate diagrams, strange symbols, and instructions written in a flowing hand. One passage caught her eye:

The star-touched must learn to release earthly tethers. Each memory held too tightly is a chain binding you to the mortal plane. To touch the infinite, you must first empty yourself of the finite. Begin with something small. A happy memory from childhood. Feel its warmth, then let it drift away like smoke. You will not forget it happened, but you will no longer feel its hold.

Elara thought of Oakhaven. Of her grandmother's cottage. Of the simple life she'd left behind. Part of her ached for it. But another part recognized that she could never go back to being that girl. Too much had changed. She had changed.

Was Seraphina right? Did she need to let go of the past to fully embrace her future?

Or was Kaelen right that those memories were what kept her grounded? What kept her human?

Eleven days until the Solstice. Eleven days to decide who she needed to become.

And with each passing day, the distance between her and Kaelen seemed to grow wider, as if some invisible force was determined to push them apart just when they needed each other most.

Chapter 7

The weight of prophecy had become almost unbearable. The opulent halls of the castle, once a stage for Elara's growing understanding of courtly life, now felt like a gilded cage. Every whisper and furtive glance reminded her of the cosmic stakes. Sleep offered no escape. Her dreams became a fractured tapestry of crumbling veils and predatory eyes, jolting her awake with a racing heart.

She sought solace in the library, a sanctuary of aged parchment and arcane lore. The tome *The Weaver's Reckoning* had become her constant companion. Its chilling accounts of those touched by starlight served as stark warnings. The prophecy's demand for unwavering intent, tempered understanding, and resolute will felt like an impossible standard for a heart still wrestling with its own tempest.

Eleven days. Eleven days until the Solstice. The countdown had become a drumbeat in her mind, relentless and unforgiving.

The fear of failure gnawed at her constantly. She scrutinized every reaction, every fleeting emotion, terrified that a momentary lapse might ripple through the Veil. Kaelen's increasing distance, his absorption in the kingdom's defenses, left her adrift in her internal war.

A passage from the tome caught her attention: *"The Veil is a living thing, woven not of substance but of balance. It is the sum of all that separates and all that connects. To mend it is to understand the profound interconnectedness of all things. To shatter it is to embrace the illusion of separation."*

The phrase "illusion of separation" struck a chord. Was her fear of inadequacy, her fixation on the chasm between who she was and who she needed to be, part of that illusion? She reached for calm, for the inner peace Kaelen had spoken of, trying to see the starlight not as a threat but as part of the natural order.

Could she find that balance? Could she hold both destruction and salvation within her without succumbing to either?

The fear remained, but a flicker of defiance ignited. She would not be defined by the prophecy's terrifying potential. She would seek understanding, not only to avoid disaster but for self-discovery.

Kaelen found her in the library three days later, when the Solstice was merely a week away. He looked haggard, the strain of preparation evident in every line of his face. But his eyes softened when they landed on her.

"Come with me," he said quietly. "I know a place that might help."

He led her away from the ornate halls, along winding paths that sank into an emerald embrace, until the cacophony of courtly intrigue gave way to the gentle symphony of nature. They emerged into a clearing bathed in ethereal, dappled light.

"This is the Heartwood Grove," Kaelen said, his low voice a balm against her anxieties.

The trees were unlike any Elara had seen. Their trunks were impossibly wide, their bark a tapestry of deep, ancient grooves that seemed to hold the wisdom of millennia. These were not mere trees but sentinels, with gnarled branches lifting like the arms of slumbering giants. Their leaves, a living emerald, whispered secrets on the breeze.

The air was thick with primal energy, a tangible peace that seeped into Elara's bones and chased away the shadows of her worry. It stood in stark contrast to the stagnant magic that sometimes pervaded the Unseelie realm. Here the magic was pure, untamed, and deeply healing.

"This grove is part of the Faewild that remains untouched by decay," Kaelen explained. "The Heartwood trees are said to be the oldest living beings in existence, their roots anchored to the very heart of the world."

He approached one of the giants and rested his hand on its rough bark. Elara followed, drawn by an inexplicable pull, a sense of homecoming that resonated deep within her.

As her fingers brushed the ancient wood, a wave of profound calm washed over her. The tree seemed to breathe, a slow, steady rhythm that mirrored her heart but deeper and steadier. The whispers of leaves overhead gathered into a gentle song about resilience, connection, and the enduring strength of life.

The weight of the prophecy began to recede like a tide pulled by an unseen moon.

"The magic here is bound to the natural world," Kaelen said softly, reverent. "It is a magic of growth, renewal, and balance. I thought you might find clarity here."

Elara nodded, unable to voice the swell of emotion rising in her. The presence of these ancient beings, their silent testimony to the passage of eons, was a potent antidote to the frantic urgency of her situation. They had witnessed countless seasons, the rise and fall of empires, the ebb and flow of magic. Still they remained, steadfast and serene.

She walked deeper into the grove, her steps lighter than they had been in weeks. The ground was a soft carpet of moss and fallen leaves. Sunlight filtered through the canopy, casting patterns of light and shadow. Tiny iridescent motes drifted lazily, like fallen stars.

She found a moss-covered stone nestled among the roots of a majestic tree. Sitting, she closed her eyes and let the grove's peace envelop her. She focused on the gentle hum that permeated the space, the quiet thrumming that felt like the pulse of the world.

She began to visualize the starlight within her, not as a capricious danger but as part of the same natural flow. The ancient trees offered a blueprint for balance. Their roots plunged deep for stability while their branches reached outward for light and air. Grounded and reaching, they held a harmony of steadiness and growth.

The leaf-whispers intensified into a collective consciousness, a symphony of ancient knowledge. They spoke of the cycles of life and death, of endings that allow new beginnings, and of the resilience inherent in all living things. They spoke of patience, allowing processes to unfold without frantic interference.

Elara felt a connection form, not only to the grove but to the essence of her own power. She had focused so long on destruction and the fear of shattering the Veil that she had missed the capacity for creation and balance within the starlight.

Time seemed to lose meaning in the grove's embrace. When she finally opened her eyes, Kaelen was sitting nearby, watching her with an expression she couldn't quite read.

"Seven days," he said quietly. "Seven days until the Solstice."

The reminder brought reality crashing back, but it no longer felt quite so overwhelming. "I had a vision," Elara said. "The grove showed me something."

She described what she had seen: the Veil as it was meant to be, a magnificent tapestry of starlight and moonlight, alive and rhythmic, the sustaining heart of both mortal and Fae realms. The harmonious exchange between worlds. And then the decay, the breaking, the pain of imbalance.

"But there was more," she continued. "I saw threads of golden light, woven with understanding and empathy, knitting the Veil back together. The prophecy isn't about choosing between destruction and preservation. It's about restoration. About healing what has been broken."

Kaelen's expression shifted, hope kindling in his silver eyes. "You've found the key," he said. "Not domination or sacrifice, but connection. Balance."

He stood and moved to one of the ancient trees, placing his palm against its bark. "There's something I need to show you."

At his touch, a faint, pearlescent mist began to gather. It coalesced into a small, glowing orb that pulsed with soft light and warmth. "This is life magic," Kaelen explained. "The essence of the Heartwood trees. It mends wounds, wards decay, and restores balance."

Elara approached, drawn by the orb's gentle radiance. When she extended her own hand to the tree, the magic responded immediately, flowing to her more readily than it had to Kaelen. Another orb formed, brighter than the first.

"You have a gift," Kaelen said, wonder in his voice. "The ability to coax this energy without force. It reflects your connection to the natural world, the very connection the curse seeks to sever."

Understanding dawned. "These could counter the curse."

"Precisely," Kaelen confirmed. "The curse feeds on corruption. This is its opposite. Life, unadulterated. Ordered and balanced."

For the next hours, Kaelen taught her how to deepen her bond with the grove, to feel the sap's slow pulse and the spirits' whispers, to visualize a reciprocal exchange rather than a one-way draw. Elara gathered several orbs, placing them into a pouch woven from moonpetal vine.

Each seed felt like a promise, a small ember of a larger fire.

"This is more than power," Kaelen said as they gathered their cache. "It's a symbol of the world's inherent goodness. The curse seeks to extinguish that and replace it with despair. Yet here the original light still burns. You've found a way to carry it forward."

He paused, then met her eyes directly. "This is the beginning of our true fight. Not with blades, but with life itself. These seeds can soothe afflicted lands, push back the shadow, and prove that even in deep darkness, healing waits to be nurtured."

But he also cautioned that the curse was complex, fed by twisted magic, corroded spirit, and despair. "A real remedy must address all three. The seeds could cleanse currents of magic, but their power would need to be amplified, directed, and sustained."

"We'll need channels," he said, examining a seed. "Rituals or artifacts to focus and amplify this energy. The old Fae understood how to direct natural forces. We must rediscover that knowledge."

Elara held the pouch close. The fear that had shadowed her since learning of the curse had given way to resolve. She had seen devastation, but she had also seen resilience and balance. Now she held tangible proof that hope could take physical form.

"Can these seeds break the curse?" she asked.

"Breaking it may require more than any single antidote," Kaelen said honestly. "The curse is rooted in imbalance. But these seeds can fight the symptoms, cleanse corruption, restore flow, and kindle hope. Hope is a powerful beginning. It's the catalyst for change."

He turned to face her fully, taking her hand in his. The touch was electric, sending warmth through her entire being. "Elara, I've been distant. I know that. The pressure of what's coming, the responsibility to my people... I let it push you away when I should have held you closer."

"Kaelen..."

"Let me finish," he said gently. "You are not just a tool to break the curse. You are not just the star-touched one of prophecy. You are... everything. You give me hope when I have none. You see solutions where I see only problems. You make me believe we can actually do this."

Elara's throat tightened with emotion. "I thought you were pulling away because..."

"Because I was afraid," he admitted. "Afraid of failing you. Afraid of losing you to this curse or to the machinations of my court. Afraid that my feelings for you would cloud my judgment when clarity is most needed." He squeezed her hand. "But I realize now that you are my clarity. Together, we're stronger than apart."

For a moment, the weight of prophecy and the countdown to the Solstice faded. There was only the two of them, standing in the heart of the ancient grove, holding seeds of hope.

"Seven days," Elara whispered.

"Seven days," Kaelen echoed. "And we'll face them together."

As they made their way back to the castle, the pouch of life magic seeds warm against Elara's side, she felt a shift within herself. The fear hadn't disappeared, but it no longer controlled her. She had found her purpose, her path.

And with Kaelen beside her, she believed they might actually succeed.

Chapter 8

The descent into the heart of the Unseelie realm was a journey into a place where shadows danced with ancient grace. Elara, her satchel heavy with carefully gathered seeds of healing, felt the shift in atmosphere as they moved deeper. The vibrant, emerald light of the Heartwood Grove was a distant memory, replaced by cool, phosphorescent glow of mineral veins and the faint shimmer of spectral flora clinging to cavern walls.

Kaelen, his confidence tinged with careful solemnity, led the way with practiced ease through the labyrinthine passages.

"The Council of Elders resides in the deepest chambers," he explained, voice resonating in the cavern. "They are the custodians of our history, arbiters of our laws, and keepers of the oldest magic. Their wisdom is vast, but their perspective is singular. They're bound by tradition and often resistant to anything that challenges the established order."

Elara nodded, understanding the delicate balance Kaelen had to strike. These were not advisors to be persuaded with logic alone. They were ancient beings shaped by centuries, perhaps millennia, of ruling a realm often perceived as dark and formidable.

"They'll be skeptical?" Elara ventured.

"Skeptical is a mild term," Kaelen replied with a faint smile, though his eyes remained serious. "They are ancient, and age breeds ingrained resistance to novelty. They've seen empires rise and fall, magic wane and wax. They've weathered it all by adhering to principles that have sustained our realm."

He paused, turning to face her fully. "The prophecy you spoke of, the one that hinted at a 'child of two worlds' and a 'shadow of decay,' they know it well. It's been a subject of much debate and, unfortunately, much fear for centuries. Many believe it foretells doom. Others see it as a harbinger of a new era."

Elara felt a tremor of apprehension. She was the "child of two worlds." Her very existence could be seen as a threat by those who clung to rigid definitions. "And what do they believe?"

"That's what we're about to discover," Kaelen said quietly. "Some believe the prophecy offers a solution, a way to mend what's been broken. But there are others, powerful voices, who see only the 'shadow of decay' and fear the 'child of two worlds' will hasten our end."

He gestured toward a massive archway carved into living rock, grander than any they'd passed. "This is the entrance to the Grand Conclave. Beyond lie the chambers of the Council of Elders."

As they approached, Elara noticed a shift in the ambient magic. It became denser, heavier, imbued with an almost palpable sense of age. The air hummed with dormant power. The stone of the archway was not merely carved; it seemed shaped by immense magical forces, its surface smooth and dark, absorbing light rather than reflecting it.

Stepping through was like entering another world entirely. The chamber was vast, a natural cathedral carved by time and magic, its ceiling lost in oppressive darkness. Yet the space was not entirely dark. A soft, internal luminescence emanated from the stone itself, a deep, rich amethyst hue that cast long shadows and highlighted imposing figures seated around a massive obsidian table at the center.

These were the Elders.

They were not merely old but ancient, their forms reflecting the passage of countless ages. Their skin was like aged parchment stretched over sharp, angular bones. Their eyes, when they focused on Elara, were like pools of starlight, deep and fathomless, carrying the weight of millennia. Some were cloaked in robes woven from shadows themselves, others adorned with intricate Fae jewelry that pulsed with faint internal light.

Each exuded an aura of immense power, a quiet but potent force that made the air feel heavy and charged.

There were seven of them. Kaelen bowed his head respectfully, gaze fixed on the central figure.

"My Lords and Ladies of the Council," Kaelen's voice resonated with formal respect. "I bring before you one who carries a message of great import, and a potential solution to the encroaching blight that threatens our lands."

The central figure, whose presence seemed to anchor the chamber, slowly turned their head. Their features were sharp, almost regal, etched with profound weariness. When they spoke, their voice was like wind through ancient stone, weathered but commanding.

"Kaelen, Prince of the Unseelie," the Elder intoned. "You bring a mortal before us. Into the heart of our sanctum. This is unprecedented."

"It is, Elder Moraine," Kaelen acknowledged. "But these are unprecedented times. The blight spreads. Our people suffer. And I believe Elara holds knowledge and ability crucial to our survival."

Another Elder, whose eyes burned like cold fire, leaned forward. "A mortal with knowledge superior to ours? Presumptuous."

"Not superior," Kaelen said quickly. "Different. She possesses a connection to the Veil unlike anything I've encountered. She can perceive the blight's nature in ways we cannot. And she brings seeds of healing from the Heartwood Grove, imbued with pure life magic."

A ripple of interest moved through the Council. Elara felt seven pairs of ancient eyes fix upon her with renewed intensity.

"Show us," Elder Moraine commanded.

Elara reached into her satchel with trembling hands and withdrew one of the seeds. It pulsed with soft emerald light, casting gentle radiance in the dim chamber. The Elders leaned closer, their expressions shifting from skepticism to guarded interest.

"Life magic," one Elder murmured. "Pure and uncorrupted."

"We've seen it before," another said dismissively. "It's insufficient. The blight is too deeply rooted."

"Perhaps because you've never had the right conduit," Elara said, surprising herself with her boldness. The words came before she could stop them. "The blight feeds on stagnation. On resistance to change. This magic responds to connection, to understanding. Not domination."

Silence fell. Several Elders bristled at a mortal speaking so directly. But Elder Moraine raised a hand for quiet.

"Explain," they said simply.

Elara took a breath, drawing courage from Kaelen's subtle nod. "The curse, the blight, whatever we call it, it's not just magical corruption. It's a symptom of imbalance. The Veil was meant to be a bridge between realms, not a barrier. When that balance breaks, when either side pulls too hard or walls itself off, the whole system suffers."

She held up the seed. "This carries the memory of that balance. But it needs someone who can speak to both sides. Someone who belongs to both worlds."

"The child of two worlds," Elder Moraine said softly, understanding dawning. "The prophecy speaks of you."

Before Elara could respond, a new voice cut through the chamber. Cold. Mocking.

"How convenient."

Malakor stepped from the shadows, his presence immediately shifting the energy in the room. He moved with predatory grace, eyes glittering with malice barely concealed beneath charm.

"My dear brother brings his pet mortal before the Council and claims she's the prophesied savior. How very theatrical." He turned to the Elders, spreading his hands in a gesture of reason. "Surely you see the manipulation at play? Kaelen's position is weak. His curse progresses. He brings this girl, fills her head with prophecies and purpose, and hopes you'll be swayed by sentimentality rather than wisdom."

"Watch your tongue, Malakor," Kaelen said, voice low and dangerous.

"Or what, brother?" Malakor smiled. "Will you defend her honor? Prove my point that your judgment is clouded by mortal attachments?"

The tension in the chamber ratcheted higher. Elara felt magic crackling in the air, responding to the confrontation. Six days until the Solstice. Six days until everything would come to a head. And they were wasting precious time on political games.

"Enough," Elder Moraine's voice cut through the brewing storm. "Prince Malakor, you forget yourself. This is a place of deliberation, not petty rivalry."

Malakor bowed with exaggerated courtesy but said nothing more.

Elder Moraine turned back to Elara. "You speak of balance and connection. Noble words. But words are insufficient. Can you demonstrate this connection? Can you prove your claim?"

Elara looked at Kaelen, who gave her an encouraging nod. She closed her eyes and focused on the seed in her palm, reaching out with the same sensitivity she'd used in the Heartwood Grove. But this time, she extended further, touching the ambient magic of the chamber itself.

The reaction was immediate. The seed's light intensified, spreading tendrils of emerald luminescence through the air. But more than that, Elara could feel the chamber responding. The ancient stones, the dormant magic woven into the very foundations, stirred. It recognized the life magic, recognized her as a conduit.

The Elders gasped as patterns of light began to trace across the floor, following ancient ley lines that had long since gone dormant. For a moment, the chamber blazed with renewed vitality, a glimpse of what it had been millennia ago before stagnation and fear had dimmed its glory.

Then Elara released the connection, and the light faded. But the impression remained. The proof.

"She is indeed touched by the Veil," Elder Moraine said softly. "And the life magic responds to her as it has not responded to any of us in centuries."

"This changes nothing," one of the other Elders argued. "She's still mortal. Still unpredictable. Still potentially dangerous."

"All true," a new voice agreed. Seraphina emerged from the shadows where she'd been observing silently. Her golden eyes fixed on Elara with unreadable intensity. "But danger is not always our enemy. Sometimes it's the catalyst for necessary change."

She moved to stand beside Elara, though not quite close enough to suggest alliance. "The blight grows stronger every day. Traditional methods have failed. Perhaps it's time we acknowledged that the old ways, while noble, are insufficient. Perhaps this mortal, with her unique gifts, represents an opportunity we cannot afford to dismiss."

Her words were carefully chosen, Elara realized. Seraphina wasn't endorsing her. She was positioning herself as the wise counselor who could guide both sides. As usual, the sorceress played her own game.

"We will consider this matter," Elder Moraine finally said. "Prince Kaelen, you and your... companion may retreat. We will deliberate and summon you when a decision is reached."

It was a dismissal. Kaelen bowed, and Elara followed his lead. As they left the chamber, she heard the Elders' voices rising in heated debate behind them.

In the corridor outside, Kaelen sagged against the wall. "That could have gone worse."

"Or better," Elara pointed out.

"True." He managed a tired smile. "But you were magnificent. The way you made the chamber respond... even Malakor couldn't dismiss that."

"Six days," Elara said quietly. "Six days until the Solstice, and we're still stuck waiting for approval from a council that can't decide if I'm salvation or doom."

Kaelen took her hand, intertwining their fingers. "We'll find a way. Whether they approve or not. I promise you, Elara, we will find a way."

She wanted to believe him. But with each passing day, the weight of prophecy grew heavier, and the path forward less clear. Whatever came next, she knew it would test them both to their absolute limits.

And time was running out.

Chapter 9

The heavy oak doors of the Grand Conclave groaned as they swung inward, revealing a space that was less a room and more a testament to the relentless accumulation of ages. This was not the gilded hall of pronouncements and political maneuvering, but the heart of Eldoria's collective memory: the Unseelie Archives. Even Kaelen, who had been granted limited access during his tutelage, faltered slightly at the threshold, the sheer weight of the knowledge pressing down on him. For Elara, it was a revelation a place where the whispers of her nascent power might finally find echoes.

The air inside was thick with the scent of aging parchment and dried ink, and something else ancient and faintly metallic, like the taste of forgotten magic. Towering shelves of obsidian-dark wood absorbed the ambient light as they climbed toward an impossibly high ceiling. Scrolls tied with brittle ribbons, leather-bound tomes embossed with indecipherable runes, and crystalline artifacts that pulsed with a faint inner glow filled every alcove. The silence was profound, as if it had swallowed centuries of page turns, the scratch of quills on vellum, and the hushed pronouncements of scholars long turned to dust.

Guiding them through this labyrinth of lore were the appointed guardians: three Fae scribes with sharp, austere features and eyes like polished jet. They moved with a silent, practiced grace, their robes the deep hue of twilight. Their presence was not merely supervisory; it was a constant reminder of the strictures on Elara's access. They embodied the

Council's caution, their gazes fixed on Elara a silent testament to the tenuous trust she had been granted.

"Elder Lyra has decreed that your access is limited to sectors on inter-realm studies and ancient magical anomalies," Kaelen murmured, careful not to disturb the stillness. "These scribes," he added with a subtle gesture, "will ensure you remain within those parameters. Any deviation will be reported immediately."

Elara nodded, her gaze sweeping across the vast expanse. The task ahead felt as monumental as the archives themselves. She had a key, but the lock was complex, and the door beyond led into a wilderness of uncertainty. Her purpose was clear: to find answers about the original pact, the genesis of the blight, and the true nature of her burgeoning abilities. But where to begin in such an ocean of knowledge?

The scribes led her to a large, circular chamber at the archives' heart. Alcoves lined the walls, each with a lectern and a single, carefully preserved text. Soft light diffused through enchanted crystals set in the ceiling, casting an ethereal glow.

"These are curated selections," the lead scribe said. He was a stern-faced Fae named Valerius, and his voice sounded like dry leaves. "Chosen for your stated purpose. Anything beyond these alcoves lies outside the scope of your permission."

Elara approached the nearest lectern. The manuscript was bound in the hide of a creature she could not name, its surface scarred and ancient. The script within was a flowing, lyrical form of Eldorian Fae a language she understood, though here it felt different, imbued with a deeper resonance.

As her trembling fingers touched the parchment, a faint warmth spread through her. It was not unwelcome. It was a gentle thrum, as if the words themselves were alive, stirring in response. She focused, drawing on the discipline Kaelen had instilled in her, and began to read.

The first texts spoke of the First Accord, a foundational agreement forged between the Fae of Eldoria and beings from the Veil, a time when boundaries between realms were more fluid and mutual understanding though perilous was central to coexistence. These were not tales of fear and exclusion but accounts of cautious diplomacy, of shared expeditions, and of deep respect for the unseen forces that governed existence.

Elara learned of the Veil Walkers, individuals with a natural affinity for liminal spaces whose souls resonated with the other side. They were not feared but revered as conduits and translators between worlds. The texts detailed their rigorous training, the rituals that preserved their balance, and their vital role in maintaining harmony.

One ancient scroll, its vellum brittle and yellowed, described a Fae named Lyraxis, renowned for her unparalleled communion with the Veil. Her descents were legendary, her insights profound. She investigated early signs of a growing dissonance a subtle corruption tainting the Veil's energies and manifesting as a creeping malaise that threatened Eldoria. She warned of a "shadow sickness," a corruption feeding on imbalance and discord.

As Elara read, something stirred within her, resonating with Lyraxis's words. Was this what she felt the draw and the intuitive grasp of the Veil's ebb and flow? The texts described attunement, a deep empathetic connection to the other realm's emotional and energetic currents. It matched her visions and dreams, full of alien landscapes and palpable emotions.

The scribes remained impassive, their vigilance unbroken, but Elara sensed a shift. Their shoulders eased; their breathing slowed. Perhaps these accounts, far from the forbidden sorcery

Thorne had warned against, interested them too. Perhaps they validated Eldoria's forgotten history.

Hours melted into a single stream of focus. Elara traced lines of ancient script, deciphered faded diagrams of energy flows, and absorbed fragmented accounts of the First Accord's unraveling. The texts spoke of gradual divergence growing fear within Eldoria that severed ties with the Veil. The isolation that followed diminished understanding and weakened defenses.

A frantic marginal note beside a map of inter-realm trade routes caught her eye. It spoke of a betrayal a deliberate act that shattered trust and ended the Accord. Details were vague and wrapped in allegory, but the implication was clear: the blight was not natural but the consequence of past conflict, a wound inflicted by malice.

"The curse," Elara murmured. It was more than a magical affliction. It was a scar in the fabric of existence, born of discord and misunderstanding.

She moved to another alcove. This section held arcane anomalies and historical records of magical imbalances. The texts were fragmented: scraps of papyrus and sections from lost tomes. They recorded localized disruptions throughout Eldorian history, times when ley lines faltered and ambient magic thinned often attributed to cosmic shifts or unforeseen fluctuations.

One recurring theme stood out: the "symbiotic drain." It described how imbalance in one realm could affect another, especially when a strong connection existed. The realms were breathing in tandem. If one struggled for air, the other suffered.

The idea hit Elara with force. The blight was not merely external; it was a symptom of a deeper, shared affliction. The Veil, untamed and chaotic, was not inherently malevolent but susceptible to disharmony. Eldoria's isolation had fostered that disharmony. Her connection to the Veil was not a curse but a consequence of ancient ties recklessly severed.

Deeper in the anomaly texts, a section on "Veil-born afflictions" chilled her. It described creeping apathy, a dimming of spirit, and a loss of vibrancy a "soul-fading" eroding the Fae essence. One passage detailed a form that absorbed ambient magic, leaving land barren and lifeless. It was the blight, clinical and precise.

The texts traced its origin not to chance but to deliberate corruption: a weapon forged by entities wronged or cast out from the Veil, driven by vengeance against those who severed the connection. They had twisted the Veil's chaotic energies into decay.

Elara's heart pounded. This aligned with Kaelen's theory of a weaponized blight. But who were these entities? What grievance fueled them? The texts remained vague, naming only "the forgotten," "the cast out," and "those who nursed eternal winter in their souls."

A scroll titled The Echoes of Sundering pulsed with a faint, melancholic light. It recounted the Accord's final days and a faction in the Fae Council that advocated extreme measures: a complete severing of ties with the Veil. They succeeded, initiating a ritual that closed the gates and suppressed lingering connections.

The scroll lamented the loss, describing how enforced separation disrupted the natural energy flow between realms and created a void ripe for exploitation. Certain beings, ostracized and embittered, found the perfect tool for revenge.

Elara glanced at the scribes. Valerius met her eyes, unreadable. She knew she was treading on dangerous ground.

The knowledge here could unravel centuries of accepted history.

She read on. The original pact, the Veil Walkers, the symbiotic drain, the weaponized blight together they formed a coherent, if terrifying, narrative. Eldoria's isolation had not brought safety. It created the very vulnerability the blight exploited. Her power, her connection to the Veil, was not a deviation but proof of enduring interconnectedness.

A passage in The Echoes of Sundering spoke of a lineage of Veil Walkers who resisted the severing, trying to maintain a thread of connection, only to be persecuted and driven into hiding. They possessed a unique understanding of the blight's origins knowledge later erased from lore.

Could she be their descendant? The thought was exhilarating and daunting. It would explain the innate pull she felt and the intuitive understanding that blossomed near the Veil's currents.

On the binding of The Echoes of Sundering, she noticed a small symbol: a crescent moon intertwined with a weeping willow branch. She recognized it from a fragmented dream. Her breath hitched. It felt like confirmation her abilities were linked to this lost history.

Her focus sharpened. She cross-referenced symbols and names from The Echoes of Sundering with other texts. The scribes maintained their stern facade, but she could feel their quiet attention. The urgency of her search outweighed the pressure of their scrutiny.

She found the willow sigil again in a catalog of arcane curses and countermeasures officially unrelated to inter-realm studies. It was a small defiance of the Council's limits. Valerius noted her interest with the faintest incline of his head but stayed silent.

The curse described there was vivid. It spoke of "soul-rot," a decay that began in spirit and manifested in the world, weakening magic, withering life, and consuming essence. A parasitic force feeding on despair and discord, its tendrils reached across dimensions. It was "forged in the crucible of broken oaths and vengeful hearts."

Beneath it, a hurried hand had scrawled: "The key lies not in banishing, but in understanding the severed chord."

The severed chord. The broken oath. The vengeful hearts. Everything pointed back to the Sundering and a betrayal that echoed through ages, culminating in the blight. Elara felt a growing conviction that her powers were not a threat but a potential solution. Her connection to the Veil the very thing feared by Thorne and others might be what could mend the severed chord and address the root cause.

The willow sigil tugged at her. It was not only the mark of the lost Walkers but a key a symbol of the interconnectedness that had been violently broken. Her path was not in forbidden spells but in understanding ancient bonds and finding a way to reforge them, to heal the wound between Eldoria and the Veil.

The weight of this knowledge settled on her not as a burden but as responsibility. She was no longer a pawn in a political game, but a potential inheritor of a forgotten legacy a descendant of those who once walked between worlds to keep balance. With each page, the archives revealed more, and Elara felt her power awaken, resonating with ancient whispers that yearned for healing. The journey had only begun, and while the path was perilous, it was lit by the steady glow of understanding.

The air in the Unseelie Archives thrummed with a new tension. Earlier texts had spoken of a tentative peace, but a brittle, scorched scroll hinted at a richer past: an era of unprecedented cooperation and shared magic. Boundaries blurred not from chaos but from a mutual desire for growth and discovery.

Fae artisans collaborated with mortal alchemists. Together they created wonders: luminous flora pulsing with arcane energy, tools that shaped stone with thought, and attempts to bridge the Veil through resonant harmonies of Fae song and mortal incantation. Markets bustled with beings from both realms. Academies flourished, trading elemental mastery for mathematics and engineering. The exchange of knowledge propelled both realms to new heights.

Elara traced the faded ink, struggling to reconcile this golden age with the fractured present. The parchment whispered of the Great Weaving the realms' interconnectedness at its zenith. There were tales of Fae heroes revitalizing barren mortal lands and mortal queens brokering peace among Fae clans. This was more than a pact. It was symbiosis.

Then the narrative darkened. The seeds of betrayal were sown by the union's architects. Ambitious Fae lords feared mortal influence and the dilution of ancient lineages. They whispered about the instability of mortal lifespans and the crude unpredictability of mortal magic. Names were obscured by codes, but their intent was clear: reclaim sole dominion.

In mortal courts, fear grew as well. Some leaders, unnerved by Fae power, advocated separation to avoid subjugation. Their anxieties, fanned by those same Fae lords, hardened into policy. Clandestine pacts promised security in exchange for severing the Weaving.

The betrayal was slow. Shared artifacts became guarded

secrets. Scholars turned wary. Exchanges faded to observation, then hostility. Amid rising distrust, the plan to seal the Veil emerged. After a violent border skirmish likely engineered Eldorian leaders proposed a radical solution: sever all connection to preserve magical integrity.

The accounts described ancient rites that tapped the fabric of dimensional boundaries. These were not the harmonious weavings of the Accord but harsh incantations fueled by fear. This dark magic was meant to seal the Veil permanently, a barrier of solidified terror and arcane force to push it back into the unknown.

The sealing was divisive. Many Fae, loyal to the Accord's wisdom, argued that isolation would create a void and fester into greater danger. Their pleas were drowned by zeal and fear.

The scroll's most harrowing detail followed: the curse on Kaelen's lineage was no natural malady. It was the sealing ritual's backlash. The unstable magic tethered itself to a specific lineage those who carried out or oversaw the rite. They bore the brunt of its recoil.

Described as a "vein of fractured essence," the curse twisted the Veil's energies and bound them to blood. It eroded the victim's connection to Eldoria's ambient magic and replaced it with a gnawing hunger for the Veil's raw power. Unfulfilled, that hunger became a wasting sickness, stealing life and essence. It was living proof of hubris a bid to control what was meant to remain intertwined.

Elara's fingers trembled. The texts spoke of creeping entropy and a whispering void that consumed from within. The leaders who sealed the Veil had created a cycle of suffering, a monument to their error.

After the sealing, the Veil's energies, warped by the failed ritual, seeped into Eldoria. The blight took shape as a direct consequence of this backfire a symptom of corrupted essence poisoning the realm. Ambition and fear had not delivered safety but a shared curse.

Knowledge of these events had been suppressed. A secret order, the Custodians of the Sundering, sought to erase records of the ritual and its fallout. They maintained the illusion of inherent strength and purity and hid that Eldoria's wound was self-inflicted.

Another set of accounts spoke of dissenters who tried to counteract the sealing's damage. Branded traitors, they worked in secret to maintain subtle connections to the Veil seeking understanding and healing. They attempted a ritual using remnants of the Accord's harmonious energies. It achieved fleeting reconnection, but the corrupted Veil and the sealing's residue caused a catastrophic backlash. The dissenters disappeared. Still, a fragment of their work survived, hidden for those brave enough to finish it.

Elara felt a deep recognition. The dissenters' purpose mirrored her own: to understand, to heal, to mend the fracture. Her resonance with the Veil was no anomaly but an echo of that lost attempt.

Clues then pointed to Lady Seraphina. Subtle records and coded letters hinted at her influence before the Sundering. They described a persuasive figure who stoked distrust and redirected resources to isolationist factions. A guarded transcript referenced a clandestine meeting where Seraphina and others discussed manipulating primal energies and harnessing fear to engineer catastrophe. The goal was not simple discord but a wound deep enough to reshape the balance between realms.

Other accounts connected Seraphina to a forbidden art

that fed on ambient fear and negative emotion. Some labeled her a patron of the Veil Breakers a secretive order bent on siphoning the Veil's raw energy. Experiments attributed to them spawned dangerous anomalies. Seraphina was portrayed as a strategist who exploited existing fractures, pushing policies that restricted contact and undermined conciliatory diplomats. Taken together, the fragments formed a dark tapestry that led to Eldoria's present suffering.

A forgotten archivist's journal proved most damning. He described Seraphina's rituals that amplified tensions and sowed distrust within Eldoria and with the Veil. He wrote of the suffocating aura of corrupted power that clung to her and of her ambition to break the Veil and harness its residue for her own ascent. His final entry, hurried and fearful, warned that her success would plunge the realm into darkness.

Elara understood the danger with chilling clarity. Seraphina was not merely a rival; she might be an architect of Eldoria's downfall.

In a hidden compartment behind ancient star charts, Elara discovered slate tablets etched with primal symbols the language of the First Ones, the oldest magic. The runes pulsed with power and unfolded a narrative through images and sensation. They described the Veil as a living tapestry woven from the essence of all realms and detailed a ritual called the Veil-mending: an act meant to heal the Veil's wounds.

This was no simple spell. It was a symphony of opposing forces life and death, light and shadow, Fae and mortal channeled not to dominate but to restore. The runes taught how to draw power from duality and balance it with alchemical precision. They described blending the first breath of a newborn, the last sigh of a dying star, the growth of a mountain, and the fury of a storm. Each element, disparate yet essential, was part of the weave.

But the tablets were incomplete. Crucial steps and incantations were missing. A recurring image hinted at a key not an object, but a living convergence of energies capable of bridging the ritual's opposites. Without it, any attempt would fail or even unravel reality.

Even so, hope surged. Here was a blueprint for healing a path to break the curse and restore balance. Elara cross-referenced the runes with forbidden fragments and reread Queen Lyra's writings. Lyra's philosophy of interconnectedness seemed foundational to the ritual. Perhaps she had known of it and left clues, if not instructions.

The runes spoke of drawing strength from the balance of mortal and Fae, a union long vilified. They echoed Lyra's warnings: isolation breeds decay, and Eldoria's strength lies in connection. The Veil-mending was not only a repair of a rift but a restoration of a relationship.

One cracked tablet described a nexus where ley lines converged a place to amplify the ritual. Elara thought of the Whispering Peaks, shrouded in myth and said to thin the veil between worlds. The description fit.

Intention mattered. The rite demanded a heart seeking true balance and a soul desiring harmony for all realms, not personal gain. Elara felt ready for that burden.

Patterns emerged as she studied. The Veil was cyclical; the Sundering was a disruption, not an ending. The ritual aimed to restart a natural process of renewal. A final spiral symbol represented completion, but faint lines around it suggested deliberate sabotage. Someone had obscured the path. Seraphina's name rose unbidden.

"Life and death" here was not necromancy but

transformation the cycle that feeds life. "Light and shadow" was not about erasing darkness, but acknowledging its role. By forcing imbalance and chasing eternal light, Eldoria had stumbled into a different kind of darkness.

The key, the last tablet implied, was a living embodiment of unity a bridge between worlds that could resonate with both realms, understand both, and bring them into accord. Not an artifact, but a person or destiny intertwined with Eldoria and the Veil.

The realization struck with terrifying clarity. The ritual was not a relic but an answer. With the missing pieces and the key, Eldoria could heal. Lyra's words had not been only philosophy; they were the ritual's principles. It felt as if she had foreseen the need and left a path to follow.

The road ahead was uncertain. The gaps were real, and the key remained unknown. The ritual was complex and demanded precision and purity. Yet, for the first time since entering the archives, Elara felt true hope. The runes were a promise that even the deepest wounds could mend. She would not rest until the Veil was mended and Eldoria was free. The weight of the discovery was immense, but she carried it with new strength, guided by wisdom etched in stone and the steady pulse of possibility.

Chapter 10

The ritual had begun.

Elara stood at the center of the tower, the stars wheeling overhead in their perfect Solstice alignment. The Council of Elders sat in their circle, watching with hawk-like intensity. Courtiers pressed at the edges, hungry for spectacle. And beside her, Kaelen stood tall despite the exhaustion etched into every line of his face.

She could feel it. The power building as the celestial bodies aligned. The Veil responding, growing thinner, more malleable. The pouch of Heartwood seeds at her belt pulsed with warmth, ready to channel.

"Now," Elder Moraine intoned. "Begin."

Elara reached into the pouch and withdrew the seeds, cradling them in her palms. They glowed with soft emerald light, pure and untainted. She closed her eyes and reached out with her awareness, touching the Veil itself.

It responded immediately. The barrier between realms shivered, acknowledging her presence. She could feel the wound, the corruption left by the Sundering. Centuries of festering damage, of broken connections and twisted magic. The blight was not a separate entity but the Veil's own pain made manifest.

"I see it," she whispered. "The tear where they sealed it. Where they severed the connection."

Kaelen moved closer, placing his hand on her shoulder. His

touch grounded her, kept her from being swept away by the immensity of what she was sensing. "Can you heal it?"

"I don't know," Elara admitted. "It's so much worse than I thought. The damage goes so deep."

She began to channel the life magic from the seeds, pouring it into the Veil. The emerald light spread, touching the corrupted edges, trying to soothe and mend. For a moment, it seemed to work. The Veil's pulse steadied. The blight recoiled slightly.

Then something pushed back.

Elara gasped as a wave of malevolence crashed into her awareness. This wasn't just corruption. It was intelligence. Purpose. The blight had been feeding on the Veil's pain for so long that it had developed a consciousness of its own. And it did not want to be healed.

"It's fighting me," she said through gritted teeth. "It doesn't want to let go."

"Then force it," Elder Thorne commanded. "Prove your power."

But forcing it would only make things worse. Elara could feel that instinctively. This wasn't a battle to be won through domination. It required understanding. Compassion. The very things the Sundering had lacked.

She shifted her approach, trying to communicate with the blight. Trying to show it that healing didn't mean destruction. That there could be balance again. Connection without exploitation.

The blight hesitated, as if considering. Then it struck back with renewed fury.

Pain lanced through Elara's skull. She felt the Veil beginning to tear further, her attempt to heal it paradoxically making things worse. The seeds in her hands began to crack, unable to handle the strain.

"Elara!" Kaelen's voice, sharp with fear.

"I can't," she gasped. "It's too strong. I'm not strong enough."

The words tasted like ash in her mouth. After everything, after all the preparation and sacrifice, she was failing. The Council had been right to doubt her. She was just a mortal girl playing at powers she couldn't understand.

The Veil began to unravel faster.

"Stop her!" Elder Moraine commanded. "She's making it worse!"

Two guards moved forward, but Kaelen stepped between them and Elara, his blade drawn. "Stay back."

"Prince Kaelen, stand aside," Elder Thorne demanded. "She is destroying what we sought to preserve."

"She's trying to heal it!" Kaelen shouted back, his control finally, completely shattering. "Can't you see that? For centuries, you've sat in your chambers, doing nothing while the blight spread! You've clung to your traditions and your purity, and all it's done is make us weaker! Elara is the first person to actually try to fix this, and you want to stop her because she might fail?"

"Your attachment to this mortal has clouded your judgment," Elder Moraine said coldly.

"My attachment?" Kaelen laughed, a wild, broken sound. "Yes, I'm attached to her. I love her. Does that scandalize you?

A Fae prince loving a mortal? Good! Maybe we need more scandal. Maybe we need less purity and more humanity!"

He turned to face the full Council, and Elara could see years of suppressed emotion flooding to the surface. Every compromise, every denied feeling, every moment of control finally breaking free.

"My entire life, I've done what you wanted," Kaelen continued, voice raw. "I've been the perfect prince. I've followed every rule. I've carried the burden of this curse with dignity and grace. And where has it gotten us? The blight spreads. My people suffer. My brother plots against me with your tacit approval because you're too afraid to choose sides!"

"Prince Kaelen..." Elder Moraine began.

"No!" Kaelen cut them off. "You'll listen to me now. You've had centuries to fix this. Centuries. And all you've done is debate and deliberate while the realm dies around you. Elara has been here for mere weeks, and she's accomplished more than any of you combined. She found the Heartwood seeds. She uncovered the truth about the Sundering. She's risked everything to save a realm that isn't even her own!"

His hands were shaking, Elara realized. Not from fear, but from the sheer force of emotion he'd kept bottled for so long.

"And you want to kill her," Kaelen said, voice dropping to something dangerous. "Because she might fail. Because she's not Fae. Because she threatens your comfortable world of tradition and stagnation." He looked around at the assembled courtiers, many of whom couldn't meet his eyes. "Well, I'm done with your comfort. I'm done with your traditions. If they haven't saved us yet, they never will."

He turned back to Elara, who was still struggling to hold the Veil together. "Tell me what you need."

"I need," Elara gasped, "someone who understands both sides. Someone who can bridge the gap. The blight isn't just corruption. It's grief. It's the Veil's pain made manifest. And it won't heal until someone acknowledges that pain. Until someone apologizes."

Understanding dawned in Kaelen's eyes. "The bloodline that created the curse."

"Has to be the one to break it," Elara finished.

Kaelen didn't hesitate. He placed his hands over hers, his silver eyes burning with determination and something deeper. Love. Absolute, unwavering love.

"Then we do it together."

He began to speak, his voice carrying across the tower and beyond, into the Veil itself. "I am Kaelen, Prince of the Unseelie, heir to the bloodline that sealed you. And I am sorry. I'm sorry for the pain inflicted. I'm sorry for the severing. I'm sorry for centuries of isolation and suffering."

His voice cracked. "You were meant to be a bridge, not a barrier. A connection, not a wound. And my ancestors, in their fear, violated that. They hurt you. And I'm sorry."

The Veil shuddered. Elara could feel it listening, really listening, for the first time.

"I can't undo what was done," Kaelen continued. "But I can try to make it right. I can choose connection over isolation. I can choose love over fear. I can choose to bridge the gap my ancestors created." He looked at Elara. "With her help. If you'll allow it."

For a long moment, nothing happened. Then, slowly, the blight began to recede. Not disappearing, but pulling back. Calming. The Veil's pulse steadied.

Elara poured the life magic from the seeds into that opening, and this time, the Veil accepted it. The emerald light spread, knitting torn edges, soothing corrupted threads. The healing had begun.

But it wasn't complete. It couldn't be, not in one night. The damage was too extensive. But it was a start. A foundation upon which true mending could build.

When the Solstice alignment finally passed and the ritual's power faded, Elara sank to her knees, exhausted. Kaelen caught her before she could fall.

"You did it," he whispered.

"We did it," she corrected.

Elder Moraine stood, face unreadable. "The ritual is... incomplete. But the blight has receded. For now."

"For now is enough," Kaelen said firmly. "We've proven it can be done. The rest will take time. Work. Continued connection between realms." He met each Elder's gaze in turn. "Are you finally ready to embrace that? Or will you cling to your failing traditions until there's nothing left to preserve?"

The silence that followed was heavy. Then, finally, Elder Moraine inclined their head. "Your point is... taken, Prince Kaelen. We will... consider new approaches."

It wasn't enthusiastic support. But it was a crack in centuries of rigid thinking. A beginning.

As the crowd dispersed and the Council withdrew to deliberate, Kaelen helped Elara to a quiet alcove. He was trembling, the emotional release finally catching up with him.

"I lost control," he said quietly. "In front of everyone. That was..."

"Necessary," Elara finished. "You needed to say those things. They needed to hear them."

"I told them I love you."

"I noticed." Elara smiled softly. "Do you regret it?"

"Not for a moment." Kaelen cupped her face in his hands. "I love you, Elara. Completely. Terrifyingly. You've changed everything. You've changed me."

"Good," Elara said. "Because I love you too. And I'm not going anywhere."

They kissed then, soft and sweet and full of promise. The Solstice ritual was over. The hardest battle still lay ahead. But for this moment, they had each other. And that was enough.

Chapter 11

The path leading to the Moonstone Caverns grew progressively darker, the canopy above becoming an impenetrable shroud. Yet a different kind of light began to assert itself, a soft, pearlescent glow that seemed to bloom from the earth itself. Elara and Kaelen felt the shift in the ambient magic, a potent, raw energy thrumming beneath the surface.

"This is the place," Kaelen murmured, his hand on his sword. "The energy is untamed. Like nothing I've felt before."

The entrance to the Moonstone Caverns was not a gaping maw but a subtle parting in the rock face, as if the mountain itself had exhaled. From within, a soft, ethereal glow spilled out. Stepping across the threshold felt like entering another realm entirely. The air inside was cool and still, carrying a subtle, resonant hum that vibrated through their bones.

The caverns were not dark but alive with light. Countless moonstones embedded in the walls, ceiling, and floor glowed with a soft, internal radiance, casting an ever-shifting tapestry of silver and blue across the cavern walls. Each stone pulsed with its own rhythm, creating a symphony of light that was both beautiful and unnerving.

"It's breathtaking," Elara whispered, her voice barely carrying in the vast space.

"Beautiful, yes, but also dangerous," Kaelen said, his tone cautious. "The magic here is potent and unbound. The spirits said the wards are strong, woven into the stone itself. They will test the intent of anyone who seeks to claim the Heartstone."

They moved deeper into the labyrinthine passages, their footsteps muffled by a layer of crystalline dust that covered the floor like fresh snow. The path twisted and turned, branching off in multiple directions, but Elara felt drawn forward by an inexplicable pull. The Heartstone was calling to her, she realized. Guiding her toward its resting place.

The first chamber they entered was vast, and the moonstones here glowed with feverish intensity. The light pulsed in waves, casting shadows that writhed and twisted into monstrous shapes. Elara felt unease crawl up her spine as the shadows began to coalesce into forms that mirrored their deepest fears.

Before her eyes, the shadows became the creeping blight, its tendrils of decay consuming the land she loved. She saw Oakhaven withering, her grandmother's cottage crumbling to dust. She saw faces of villagers twisted in agony, accusing her of abandoning them. The images were so vivid, so real, that she gasped and stumbled backward.

Beside her, Kaelen went rigid. His silver eyes were fixed on a vision only he could see, but Elara could guess its nature from the pain etched into his features. He was seeing his ancestral lands barren and withered, his people in despair, his legacy reduced to ash and ruin.

"It is the first ward," Kaelen said, his voice tight with strain. "A ward of despair. It feeds on fear. Do not let it consume you, Elara. Remember why we are here."

Elara's breath hitched, but his words anchored her. She closed her eyes against the visions and focused on the truth beneath the illusions. These were not reality. They were possibilities, yes, but they were also what she was fighting to prevent. The visions only strengthened her resolve.

"I remember," she said, opening her eyes with new determination. "We are here to mend, not to despair."

She focused on the spirits' chant, the one they had taught her in the Whispering Woods. She visualized a restored Eldoria, lands healed and thriving, the Veil whole and strong. She projected her intent to heal, pushing it outward like a wave of light against the encroaching shadows.

The images wavered. Kaelen, sensing her strength, drew on it and joined his will to hers. He envisioned his people safe and prosperous, his kingdom renewed. Together, their combined determination created a barrier against the despair.

Slowly, the gloom receded. The monstrous shadows dissolved like mist in sunlight, revealing the chamber's true nature beneath. It was simply stone and moonstone, beautiful but no longer threatening. The ward had tested them and found them worthy.

"Well done," Kaelen said, though his voice still carried traces of the fear he'd faced. "The ward is passed."

They ventured onward, but the caverns were not finished testing them. In a wide chamber ahead, crystalline shards suddenly shot from the walls like arrows, sharp as obsidian and imbued with paralytic magic. Kaelen's sword was in his hand instantly, a silver blur as he deflected the projectiles with precise parries.

Elara reacted on instinct, calling on her connection to the Veil. A shimmering barrier formed around them, its surface rippling like water as it absorbed the remaining shards. She felt each impact drain a bit of her strength, but the barrier held.

"Second ward passed," Kaelen panted when the assault

finally ceased. "Two down. The spirits said there would be three."

"Then we're close," Elara said, though exhaustion was beginning to set in.

They pressed forward with renewed urgency. The passage opened into a vast circular chamber that took Elara's breath away. The ceiling formed a perfect dome of concentrated moonlight, as if the cavern had captured the sky itself. In the center of the chamber, suspended in the air by unseen forces, was a large, pulsating crystal that cast an intensified glow across everything.

And within its depths, nestled among swirling currents of pure arcane energy, was the Heartstone.

It was roughly the size of Elara's palm, its surface smooth and dark as midnight, yet it absorbed and refracted the chamber's light in such a way that it seemed to possess an inner luminescence. Subtle, swirling patterns played across its surface like captured moonlight dancing on water. Even from a distance, Elara could feel its power, a deep thrumming that resonated with something fundamental in her very being.

"The Heartstone," she breathed, unable to look away.

Kaelen remained tense beside her, his warrior's instincts on high alert. "It is not unguarded. The final ward is near. I can feel it."

As if in response to his words, the central crystal flared with sudden brilliance. The Heartstone's swirling patterns intensified, pulsing faster. The despair that had characterized the first ward faded, replaced by something far more insidious.

The moonstones throughout the chamber began to pulse with a warmer, more seductive light. The air grew heavy with a scent that was both intoxicating and unsettling, carrying hints of desire, not only physical but the craving for power, recognition, comfort, and control.

Images formed in the air around them, shimmering and beautiful. Elara saw herself as a revered sorceress, standing before crowds of adoring followers. Her power was unbound, limitless. She could reshape reality with a thought, command the elements with a gesture. No one would ever doubt her again. No one would ever see her as just a village herbalist. She would be legendary.

The vision was intoxicating. Every secret desire she'd ever harbored seemed to manifest before her eyes. Respect. Power. The ability to protect everyone she loved without limitation. Who wouldn't want that?

"The ward of temptation," Kaelen said beside her, his voice strained. She glanced at him and saw that he too was transfixed by his own vision. She could guess its nature: Kaelen as a king, his kingdom restored and expanded, his reign absolute. His father's approval finally earned. His brother's schemes crushed beneath his boot.

It would be so easy to reach out and take it. The Heartstone was right there, offering them everything they'd ever wanted.

But Elara remembered the spirits' warning. This was selfish power, the kind that isolated and corrupted. The Heartstone was meant to be a bridge, not a weapon. It was meant to restore balance, not tip the scales toward domination.

"This is wrong," she said aloud, as much to convince herself as Kaelen. "This isn't why we're here."

She closed her eyes against the seductive visions and focused once more on the primal chant. The words came easier now, flowing through her like a familiar song. She focused on the purpose that had brought them here: not personal glory, but healing. Not power over others, but connection between realms.

Kaelen, hearing her begin the chant, recognized what she was doing. He hardened his own resolve, pushing away the tempting visions of absolute power. He added his voice to hers, though his words were in the ancient Fae tongue, their meanings complementing her own.

As their intentions solidified and their combined will pushed outward, the seductive illusions flickered. The images of glory and power began to fade, unable to maintain their hold against such unified purpose.

The chamber's light returned to its natural, cool luminescence. The final ward had been overcome.

But they weren't safe yet. The central crystal pulsed with an intense surge of light, and the Heartstone pulsed in kind. Within its depths, a new vision formed, and this one was not an illusion or a test of will. It was a truth, stark and unavoidable.

The vision showed Elara bathed in the light of twin moons, holding the Heartstone high above her head. Beside her, Kaelen's form wavered and faded, his essence being slowly absorbed into the stone. The vision was clear in its meaning: the Heartstone could be fully awakened and imbued with the power needed to heal the Veil, but it would require a significant sacrifice. One of them would need to pour their life force into it, permanently diminishing their own existence to anchor the stone's power.

The implication was stark and terrifying. To awaken the Heartstone properly, to give it the strength it needed to mend the Veil, one of them would have to give up a part of their very essence. Not death, perhaps, but a permanent weakening. A sacrifice that could never be undone.

Elara looked at Kaelen, her heart hammering. His face showed that he had seen the same vision, understood the same terrible choice. And in his eyes, she saw determination. He was willing. He would make that sacrifice if it meant saving his realm.

"No," Elara whispered, her voice thick with emotion. She stepped toward the suspended crystal, toward the Heartstone pulsing within. "This cannot be the way."

Kaelen moved beside her, his hand warm and grounding as it covered hers. "Elara. We knew this would not be easy. The spirits warned us. The cost of mending the Veil will be great. And I am willing to give what is needed."

"But it shouldn't be you," Elara protested, tears stinging her eyes. She thought of everything he had already sacrificed, all the burdens he carried. To ask him to give up part of his essence, to diminish himself for his kingdom...

Then she thought of the primal chant, of the spirits' wisdom. They had spoken of balance, of weaving together disparate elements. They had spoken of partnership, of two becoming one. "Perhaps it is not about one of us sacrificing everything," she said slowly, understanding beginning to dawn. "Perhaps it is about both of us offering what we can. Together."

She turned back to the Heartstone, seeing it with new eyes. Not as a demand for ultimate sacrifice, but as an invitation to shared purpose. "Our combined will. Our connection to both realms. Our love for this world and for each other... perhaps that is the greatest offering we can make."

She placed both hands on the cool surface of the suspended

crystal, feeling the Heartstone's pulse through it. "I will offer my energy. My connection to the wild magic. My will to see the Veil healed."

Kaelen met her gaze, and she saw understanding and relief flood his features. He placed his hands over hers, their fingers intertwining. "And I offer mine. My Fae essence. My will to protect my home. My dedication to balance." He paused, then added softly, "My love for you."

"And mine for you," Elara whispered back.

A new light emanated from their joined hands, neither purely Elara's wild magic nor solely Kaelen's Fae energy, but something new. A radiant blend of silver and gold, of starlight and shadow, of mortal and Fae. The Heartstone responded to this offering, its swirling patterns beginning to still and coalesce.

The spectral images of sacrifice faded, replaced by a pure white light that pulsed with the rhythm of their intertwined heartbeats. The chamber hummed with building intensity, the moonstones vibrating in resonance. The Heartstone, infused with their shared essence rather than drained from a single source, began to pulse with steady, powerful rhythm.

They had found the third way. Not domination, not ultimate sacrifice, but partnership. Balance.

The suspended crystal slowly descended, bringing the Heartstone within Elara's reach. She carefully took it in her hands, feeling its weight and warmth. It no longer felt like an alien artifact but like something that belonged with her. A part of her.

"We did it," Kaelen said, wonder in his voice.

But their triumph was short-lived. The serenity of their

victory shattered with the sudden clang of steel on stone and guttural roars echoing through the chamber.

Malakor stood silhouetted against the Heartstone's light at the chamber's entrance, flanked by guards in obsidian armor who moved with predatory grace.

"A rather impressive display," Malakor said, his voice laced with cold amusement. His eyes gleamed with avarice as they fixed on the stone in Elara's hands. "You awakened the Heartstone. Remarkable. I must admit, brother, I underestimated you both. But in doing so, you have merely forged the weapon I shall claim."

Elara's hand tightened protectively around the Heartstone. Beside her, Kaelen moved with decisive grace, his blade appearing in his hand and blazing with defiant light.

"Malakor," Kaelen growled, positioning himself between his brother and Elara. "You dare show your face here. You've been following us."

"I've been watching everything, dear brother," Malakor said with a cruel smile. "Did you truly think I would let you keep such power? I have been daring since I first tasted this world's sweet, corrupted magic. And now..." He gestured toward the Heartstone. "Now, give me what is mine."

"It was never yours," Elara said, finding her voice despite her fear. "The Heartstone responds to balance, not domination. It will never serve you."

"We shall see about that." Malakor's smile widened. "Guards, take them."

With a nod from their master, Malakor's guards surged forward. Kaelen met the first wave with a roar, his blade becoming a silver blur of deadly precision. He was a whirlwind of Fae steel and grace, each movement economical and lethal.

A guard lunged at Elara, his blade aimed at her heart. She raised the Heartstone instinctively, and golden light flared from it, forming a shimmering shield that met the blade with a resonant clang. The guard stumbled back, momentarily stunned.

Malakor watched from his position at the entrance, eyes narrowed with calculation. "Clever," he said. "But a shield is only as strong as the hand that wields it, and you are untrained in war, little mortal."

He raised his hand, and a dark tendril of energy snaked from his fingertips toward the Heartstone. The tendril moved like a living thing, seeking and hungry.

When it struck, the golden shield wavered. Elara cried out, feeling a sickening drain as Malakor's corrupted magic tried to wrestle control of the Heartstone's power. It was like icy fingers reaching into her chest, trying to tear away the connection she had just forged.

"No!" Kaelen roared. He broke free from two guards he'd been fighting and moved to intercept another attacker who had gotten too close to Elara.

Elara saw an opening in the chaos. She focused the Heartstone's energy, remembering how it had responded to her intent earlier. She pushed its power outward in a concussive wave, not trying to control or direct it with precision, but simply releasing it in a burst of raw force.

Golden light exploded from the stone, slamming into the guards in a shockwave. They stumbled, disoriented and struggling to keep their footing. Even Malakor flinched, his dark tendril dissipating.

"Now, Kaelen!" Elara cried.

Kaelen didn't hesitate. He lunged toward a tunnel opening on the far side of the chamber that he'd spotted earlier, deflecting the lead guard's sword with a sharp parry. Ignoring the searing pain in his side from an earlier blow he hadn't had time to acknowledge, he spun and grabbed Elara's hand.

"This way! Run!"

They fled into the narrow, dark tunnel, leaving the Moonstone Chamber behind. The sounds of pursuit echoed immediately. Armor scraped against rock walls. Boots pounded against stone. Malakor's furious shouts reverberated through the passages.

"We are trapped," Elara gasped, her lungs burning. Ahead, the tunnel narrowed to what looked like an impassable crevice.

"Not yet," Kaelen said between breaths, though he was clearly weakening. He pushed forward with a surge of Fae strength, forcing his way through the narrow opening. "Come on. We can make it."

Elara plunged into the crevice after him, the rough stone scraping her arms and sides. On the other side, Kaelen helped pull her through, but she could see the pallor of his skin, the way he was breathing shallow and quick. He was hurt worse than he'd let on.

The guards were right behind them, their shouts growing closer.

Kaelen grabbed a jagged shard of obsidian from where it had fallen on the tunnel floor and hurled it back toward the crevice. It struck true, finding one of the pursuing guards. The man fell with a crunch, and his body, combined with falling debris his fall triggered, temporarily clogged the narrow passage.

"That will not hold for long," Kaelen panted, leaning heavily against the wall. He winced, his hand pressed to his side, and Elara saw dark blood seeping between his fingers.

"Kaelen, you're hurt!"

"I'm fine," he lied, but his legs were shaking. "Keep moving."

They pushed forward, the sounds of pursuit growing fainter as the guards struggled with the blockage. The passage began to slope upward, and ahead, Elara could see a crack of natural light filtering through from above. Fresh air reached them, carrying the scent of growing things.

They rounded a bend, and hope surged. The passage led to a shaft that opened to the surface. Starlight filtered through, beautiful and promising.

But a guttural roar from above froze them in their tracks.

One of Malakor's beasts, a creature of shadow and fang that looked like a wolf but stood tall as a horse, waited at the top of the shaft. Its eyes glowed with malevolent intelligence.

"No," Elara breathed, raising the Heartstone defensively.

Kaelen pushed her behind him, sword drawn despite his obvious exhaustion. His movements were sluggish, his grip on his weapon uncertain. "Go, Elara. Climb past it. Get to the surface. Warn the others."

"I will not leave you!" Elara's voice cracked with desperation.

"You must," Kaelen commanded, though his voice was gentle. "The Heartstone is more important than either of us. It must reach safety. I'll hold the beast off."

The creature began its descent, claws finding purchase on the rocky walls. Its massive jaws opened, revealing teeth like daggers.

Kaelen met the beast's charge with a desperate cry. His sword flickered in the dim light, finding the creature's shoulder. But claws tore through his armor in response, raking deep gashes across his chest. He staggered, blood streaming from the wounds.

"Kaelen!" Elara's scream echoed through the shaft.

He was losing. He was going to die if she didn't do something.

But the Heartstone pulsed in her hand, warm and insistent. She could feel its message: *Live. Survive. Continue the mission.*

With a sob of anguish and guilt, Elara turned and scrambled toward the opening above, clutching the Heartstone to her chest. The beast's roars and Kaelen's cries of pain followed her, each sound a knife to her heart. She pushed through the narrow gap with desperate strength and tumbled out onto soft grass under an open sky.

The moon hung high above her, full and bright. She was out. She had escaped. She was alive.

But the victory felt hollow, bitter as ash. She turned back to the opening, straining to hear anything from below. The sounds from within grew fainter, then fell silent.

The silence was worse than any scream.

Tears streamed down Elara's face, hot and bitter. Had she lost him? Had Kaelen's bravery, his sacrifice, been for nothing? She looked down at the Heartstone in her hands. Its light was soft and steady, pulsing with the combined essence they had given it.

She was in a secluded glade, surrounded by ancient trees. The place felt protected, sacred somehow. But Malakor would not stop here. He would hunt her, track the Heartstone's energy signature, and he would not rest until he claimed it.

The victory in the Moonstone Caverns, the awakening of the Heartstone, had been real. But it was only a prelude to a greater war. Malakor had shown his hand, revealed the depths of his ambition and cruelty.

Elara clutched the Heartstone close to her heart and let herself weep for a moment. Then, with shaking hands, she wiped her tears and stood. She had escaped with the Heartstone. Kaelen had given her that chance. She would not let his sacrifice be meaningless.

She would survive. She would fight. And somehow, she would find a way to save both Kaelen and the realms that depended on the Heartstone's power.

The escape was complete, but the true journey was only beginning.

Chapter 12

The cool, damp air of the glade was a balm to Elara's ravaged senses. It carried the scent of rich, untamed earth, dew-kissed leaves, and something else subtle and ancient, like the whisper of forgotten spells. She stumbled through the narrow opening, lungs burning and body aching from the rough passage, and stepped into a sanctuary of breathtaking beauty.

Sunlight, fractured into a thousand golden shards, dappled the emerald moss that carpeted the ground. Towering trees with leaves of shimmering silver formed a living canopy, their branches arching in a silent, eternal dance. The air hummed with a vibrant, protective energy, a complete contrast to the oppressive darkness and fear that had clung to her like a shroud.

She turned back, heart still hammering, just as Kaelen emerged from the crevice. He was pale, his breath coming in shallow, ragged gasps. The torn fabric of his tunic revealed raw, bleeding gashes on his chest and side. The Fae armor had done little against the beast's claws. He leaned against the rock face, his eyes, usually bright with a quick spark, now clouded with pain.

But when he saw Elara safe, a faint flicker of relief crossed his features.

"The creature," he rasped, voice strained. "It won't follow. Not easily. This glade is shielded." He pushed away from the rock, his movements stiff and pained. "Malakor's beasts sense the wardings. They hesitate."

Elara rushed to his side, her own exhaustion forgotten. She touched his blood-soaked tunic gently, and her fingers came away sticky and warm. "Kaelen, you're badly hurt."

The tears she had shed in flight threatened to return, now born of raw, unbearable anguish. She had escaped, yes, but at what cost? The silence from the tunnel behind them roared in her ears. She had left him to face that creature alone.

He managed a weak smile, a shadow of his usual charm. "A few scratches, Princess. Nothing I haven't endured."

"Don't call them scratches," Elara said, her voice breaking. "You're bleeding too much. You could have died back there. You almost..."

"But I didn't," Kaelen interrupted gently. He winced as he straightened, a hand pressed to his side. "Though perhaps this one is deeper than usual." He looked around at the glade with quiet appreciation, as if trying to distract himself from the pain. "My mother called this place Eldoria's Cradle. A sanctuary, hidden from the world. She brought me here when I was a child, when court pressures grew heavy. The magic here soothes. It heals."

He took a hesitant step, then another, leaning heavily on Elara's shoulder as they moved deeper into the glade. The moss cushioned their steps, soft as velvet. The silver leaves caught the sunlight and seemed to amplify it, casting a gentle, ethereal glow that made the whole space feel otherworldly.

Strange, luminous flowers bloomed in scattered clusters, their petals like spun moonlight and their scent sweet and intoxicating. The air itself seemed alive with magic, pure and ancient, wrapping around them like a protective embrace.

"Can you truly heal here?" Elara asked, hope threading through her voice despite her fear. She guided him to a fallen log draped in velvety moss, helping him sit. He sank onto it with a low groan that made her heart clench.

The Heartstone pulsed gently in her hand, its warmth comforting, its thrum deeper now, as if answering the glade's ancient magic.

Kaelen nodded, closing his eyes for a moment. When he opened them again, she could see him struggling to focus through the pain. "The ambient magic is potent. Pure Fae magic, untainted by corruption or politics. It amplifies our natural healing, but it will take time. And assistance."

His gaze steady despite the pain, he continued, "You must be exhausted. And frightened. You faced the caves, the wards, the pursuit, the beast. You showed remarkable courage back there, Elara. More courage than most warriors I know."

Elara shook her head vehemently. "It was you. You fought for me. You kept them back." Her voice cracked at the memory of his struggle against the beast, the sound of claws tearing through armor, his cry of pain. "I should have stayed. I should have helped you fight instead of running."

He reached for her with his uninjured hand, finding hers and gripping it firmly. His skin was cool from blood loss, yet his grip was sure and steady. "You did what you had to do. You escaped with the Heartstone. That was your task, the most important one. Mine was to see you through, to give you that chance." He squeezed her hand. "These wounds are the price of success. And I would pay it again, a thousand times, to see you safe."

A wave of emotion washed over Elara, so powerful it nearly overwhelmed her. Relief that he was alive, grief at what he'd endured, fear of what still might happen, and beneath it all, a love so deep it ached in her chest. She knelt beside him, carefully tracing the edge of one of the deep gashes with a feather-light touch.

"This is more than a few scratches," she said, her voice barely above a whisper. "You're bleeding too much. We need to stop it."

"Fae resilience is a remarkable thing," he said, though his voice was weaker now. "We endure much that would kill a mortal. And this place will help. It holds old magic that mends bone and spirit. But it needs focus. A channel to direct its power."

His gaze fell to the Heartstone in her hand. Its light, which had been vital to their escape, now cast a softer, gentler glow, as if harmonizing with the glade's own magic. "The Heartstone's connection to the earth and to older power makes it an excellent conduit. It can amplify the glade's restorative energies, focus them. But it requires a strong will and focused intent from the wielder."

Elara understood what he was asking. The Heartstone was not only a source of power but a tool that answered to the wielder's emotions and intent. She had used it for protection and defense, had felt its power surge through her in moments of desperation. But healing on this scale? That was different. More delicate. More precise.

"I don't know if I can," she whispered, looking down at the stone. "My magic is still new to me. I've only begun to understand it, to control it. What if I make it worse? What if I hurt you?"

Kaelen's thumb stroked the back of her hand in a soothing rhythm. "You wielded it with perfect control in the tunnels.

You unleashed a wave of force that repelled Malakor's soldiers without harming me. That was no small feat. You have more power and more control than you give yourself credit for."

He paused, his breath catching as another wave of pain washed over him. When he spoke again, his voice was softer, more intimate. "And you have something even stronger than magic: love. Love for your people, for your home, and..." he hesitated, then continued, "for those you care about."

His gaze lingered on her face, and the unspoken words hung between them, as clear as if he'd shouted them. "Let that guide you. Let the Heartstone focus your intent. Trust it, and trust yourself."

He shifted slightly, and she saw him wince as fresh pain lanced through him. "We should staunch the bleeding first, then try to close the wounds. But before that..." He met her eyes directly. "Could you try? For me?"

Elara looked at the Heartstone, then at his pale, pained face. She saw not only a wounded prince, not only a warrior who had saved her life, but the man she had come to love. The man who believed in her when she doubted herself. She couldn't let his sacrifice be in vain. She couldn't let him suffer when she might have the power to help.

She drew a deep breath, trying to center herself despite the exhaustion and fear. Closing her eyes, she focused on the Heartstone's steady warmth in her palm. She pictured Kaelen as she wanted him to be: strong and whole, his wounds closed and his pain eased. She poured all her love and urgency into the stone, imagining it as a channel for the glade's healing magic.

Energy surged in response, vibrant and alive, flowing through her in a rhythm that matched the glade's own pulse. The Heartstone brightened in her hand, its golden light beginning to swirl and mix with the glade's silvery glow, creating something new and beautiful.

She opened her eyes and carefully held the Heartstone over Kaelen's worst wound. The light coalesced, becoming almost tangible, like a veil of liquid gold that settled gently over the torn flesh. Kaelen gasped, the sound part pain and part wonder.

Elara felt her own energy beginning to drain, a deep fatigue pressing in at the edges of her consciousness, but she held fast. With her mind's eye, she could almost see the energy flowing from the Heartstone into Kaelen's body, weaving through damaged tissue, mending torn muscle, sealing ruptured veins.

The bleeding slowed, then stopped entirely. The edges of the gashes began to knit together, the redness fading to a healthier pink. It was working. It was actually working.

Slowly, Kaelen touched his chest with trembling fingers. His eyes widened with amazement. "Elara," he breathed, his voice filled with awe. "You did it. You actually did it."

Elara sagged against him, her strength completely spent. The Heartstone dimmed to a gentle pulse in her hand. "It was the glade," she whispered, her voice exhausted. "And you. Your belief in me."

Kaelen drew her close with his uninjured arm, cradling her against his chest. She could hear his heartbeat, strong and steady now. "It was your will, your power, and your love," he corrected gently. "Never doubt that."

He held her as the glade's quiet peace returned around them. The silver leaves whispered in a breeze that carried comfort and safety. For a long moment, they simply sat together, drawing strength from each other's presence.

After a while, Kaelen spoke again, his voice stronger though still tired. "We cannot stay here forever. Malakor won't give up. He's relentless when he wants something, and he wants the Heartstone more than anything. He will search for us. He will sense the Heartstone's energy, even if he can't pinpoint its exact source. This glade protects us, but it isn't a fortress."

Elara pulled back slightly, forcing herself to think about practical matters despite her exhaustion. The immediate danger had passed, but the larger threat remained. "What do we do?"

"We rest first," Kaelen said firmly. "We both need it. Then we heal more completely, take stock of what supplies we have, and choose our course." His expression grew grim. "Returning to the palace now would be too dangerous. Malakor will have reinforcements there, and his spies are everywhere in the court. We need somewhere to lie low, to recover our strength and plan our next move."

He touched his wounds, which were now mostly healed but still tender. "The glade's enchantments are potent but subtle. They mask our presence, blur our location, but they don't make us invisible. If Malakor's forces come close enough, they'll feel the disturbance in the natural magic. We must be ready to move quickly if needed."

He nodded toward the Heartstone, which rested now in Elara's lap, its soft glow steady and reassuring. "This is the key to everything. Malakor craves it above all else. We must protect it at all costs. And if it can heal like this, imagine what else it might be capable of."

Elara lifted the Heartstone, feeling its familiar weight and the subtle thrumming of power within. It felt different now, somehow. More connected to her. More responsive. "The spirits said very little about its full capabilities. They spoke of balance, of bridging realms, of mending what was broken. But they didn't explain how."

"Then we'll learn together," Kaelen said. "We have time now, at least a little. We should use it wisely."

They spent the next hours tending to Kaelen's remaining injuries with more mundane methods. Elara discovered a small satchel he had managed to keep with him during their flight. Inside were a few dried rations, a waterskin, and, most importantly, a pouch of herbs she recognized as potent Fae salves.

Her mother had taught her about healing, had passed down knowledge of plants and their properties. Those teachings, which Elara had once thought quaint and old-fashioned, now became a lifeline. She untied the pouch, releasing the earthy aroma of crushed leaves and roots. There were sprigs of Moonpetal for soothing and drawing out infection, and slivers of Sunstone root, a strong astringent that would staunch any remaining bleeding and speed regeneration.

"This is quite the collection," Kaelen murmured, watching her work with appreciation. Despite his weakened state, there was warmth in his gaze.

"My mother believed in preparation," Elara said, her voice soft with memory. "She said even the strongest magic benefits from the earth's wisdom." She mixed the herbs into a paste with a few drops of water from the skin, creating a fragrant balm.

"Your mother was wise," Kaelen said with quiet reverence. "I remember stories of her, even in my court. She was known as a woman of great spirit and greater healing skill."

Elara's throat tightened at the mention of her mother. She had lost her years ago, and the pain had never fully healed. But now, using her mother's teachings to save Kaelen, she felt a connection across that divide. A sense that her mother would have approved of this choice, this path.

She began to clean his wounds more thoroughly, using a soft cloth dipped in Moonpetal-infused water. Kaelen flinched but didn't pull away. "Easy," she whispered, her touch as gentle as possible.

As she worked, her fingers brushed against his skin, and she became acutely aware of the intimacy of the moment. His skin was cool and smooth where it wasn't marred by wounds, and she could feel the steady rhythm of his pulse beneath her fingertips.

"You have a healer's touch," Kaelen said softly, his voice a little stronger now. "It's comforting."

She glanced up and found him watching her with an intensity that made her breath catch. His eyes, usually so carefully guarded in court, were open and vulnerable now. The attraction that had simmered between them since their first meeting had deepened in this sanctuary's quiet intimacy. Far from court politics and societal expectations, they were simply two souls relying on each other to survive.

"I'm just trying to make you comfortable," she murmured, feeling a blush warm her cheeks.

"Kaelen," he corrected gently. "Please. We're beyond formalities, Elara. Here, we're just... us."

She nodded, unable to speak past the emotion tightening her throat. She applied the Sunstone paste carefully, and slowly, methodically, she laid the herbal poultices over each wound. The pungent herbs mingled with the glade's sweet perfume, creating a scent that was both earthy and otherworldly.

She felt the glade's gentle warmth seeping into him through the treatments, speeding his natural Fae healing even further.

With each careful touch, she felt the bond between them growing deeper, forged in shared peril and tender care.

"You are remarkably strong," she said softly, not quite able to meet his eyes. "To fight so fiercely when you were already wounded. To face that beast alone."

"I would do it again," he said, and when she looked up, his eyes were holding hers with an intensity that stole her breath. "A thousand times, if it kept you safe."

He reached out and laced his fingers with hers, his touch sending a warm shiver through her entire body. "You risked everything to retrieve the Heartstone. Your courage in the face of such darkness is extraordinary. You are extraordinary."

His words steadied her frayed nerves, but they also sharpened her awareness of the forbidden nature of her feelings. He was a Fae prince, and she was... what? A mortal with strange powers she barely understood. A village herbalist thrust into a world of magic and prophecy. Their worlds were so different, and yet here, in this moment, none of that seemed to matter.

"We did what we had to do," she whispered, but she didn't pull her hand away from his. His grip was gentle yet sure, a silent promise of protection and something more.

"And now, we rest," Kaelen said, his eyes drifting to the dappled light filtering through the silver leaves. "We let this place do its work. Then we decide our next move. But Elara..." He squeezed her hand. "Whatever comes next, we face it together. Agreed?"

"Agreed," she whispered.

As night fell over the glade, they made camp beneath the ancient trees. The Heartstone provided a soft, warm light, and the glade's protective magic wrapped around them like a blanket. Elara found herself leaning against Kaelen's shoulder, his arm around her, and for the first time since this journey began, she felt something like peace.

Tomorrow would bring new challenges. Malakor was still out there, hunting them. The fate of realms still hung in the balance. But tonight, in Eldoria's Cradle, they were safe. And they were together.

That was enough.

Chapter 13

Whispers reached them on the currents of magic that clung to the Cradle, furtive echoes of Malakor's schemes carried on threads of corrupted power. Kaelen, his senses attuned to the subtler shifts in the Faewild's energies, confirmed what Elara had begun to sense through her connection to the Heartstone.

"He is not idle," Kaelen said, his voice tight with suppressed anger. "He's already begun spinning his narrative. He's twisted the attack on us in the Moonstone Caverns into something else entirely. He calls it defiance against weakness, a necessary strike against my supposed treachery."

"Treachery?" Elara asked, a chill running through her despite the glade's warmth. "We were attacked. We fled to survive. How is that treachery?"

"To Malakor, your very flight proves guilt," Kaelen explained, his jaw clenched. "And my presence with you, my defense of you, proves I'm aligned with your failings. He's using this to consolidate power in the Unseelie Court. He paints himself as the strong hand that's needed, while portraying me as a pawn swayed by a mortal's influence."

His gaze hardened as he spoke, anger and frustration bleeding through his usual control. "He's fanning old resentments, stoking fears that have simmered in the court for centuries. The Unseelie nobles are volatile and ambitious by nature. He exploits their fear and greed with surgical precision."

The Heartstone pulsed faster in Elara's hand, as if sensing the gathering darkness they discussed. She brushed its smooth surface with her thumb, finding comfort in its steady warmth. It felt alive, aware. A beacon of hope, yes, but also a target that drew danger like a lodestone.

"What does he hope to achieve?" she asked, though she feared she already knew the answer.

"Control," Kaelen said simply. "Absolute control. He seeks the throne, Elara. He always has. But he knows that the Heartstone, properly wielded and in its rightful place, can bind the realms together and stop his ambitions cold. So he must get to it first. He must corrupt it, twist it into his weapon rather than allow it to be used for healing."

He paused, his expression growing grimmer. "There are rumors he's seeking darker alliances. Forbidden pacts."

Elara's heart sank. "What kind of alliances?"

"The worst kind," Kaelen said, barely contained anger evident in every word. "Pacts with entities that thrive on chaos and decay. Ancient things that should remain forgotten. He's delving into rituals that haven't been performed in millennia, trying to augment his own power. He doesn't just want to be a prince or even a king. He wants to become something more. A force of nature. A harbinger of his own dominion over both our realms."

He scanned the tranquil glade as if the very trees might be listening, might carry his words to unfriendly ears. "His urgency suggests he knows time is working against him. He fears the Veil-mending ritual. If we perform it successfully with the Heartstone, his path to power closes forever. So he's racing against time. Racing against us."

Fear trembled through Elara's body, but beneath it, resolve

burned hot and fierce. She had not come this far, sacrificed this much, to let a power-hungry tyrant plunge their worlds into darkness.

"He cannot be allowed to succeed," she said firmly, her voice carrying a strength she hadn't known she possessed. "He would plunge both our realms into an eternal twilight just so he could rule over the ashes."

"Exactly," Kaelen said, covering her hand where it rested on the Heartstone. His touch was warm, grounding, real. "His ambition threatens not just you and the stone, but the very fabric of existence. The old prophecies speak of a time of great darkness, when the barriers between realms would fail and chaos would reign. He is that shadow made manifest. And he's pushing his influence further every day, testing the limits of what he can control."

He drew a steadying breath before continuing. "One of our scouts was captured by his forces recently. Before he escaped, he overheard talk of Malakor's preparations. Dark chambers where arcane energies are being channeled. Sacrifices performed under new moons. Incantations spoken in tongues so old they predate even the Fae language. All of it designed to extend his reach far beyond the Unseelie Court."

Elara absorbed the chilling picture being painted. Malakor wasn't just after the Heartstone anymore. He was trying to reshape magic itself, to corrupt its very flow and bend it to his will. The ambition was breathtaking in its scope and terrifying in its implications.

"The scout also spoke of Malakor's growing impatience," Kaelen continued. "He expected to seize the Heartstone quickly when he attacked us in the caverns. When he failed, when you awakened its power and bound it to your essence, his fury deepened. Now he seeks more potent methods, more dangerous avenues. He's becoming desperate, and a desperate Malakor is even more dangerous than a calculating one."

Elara tightened her fingers around the Heartstone, feeling its pulse steady and strong against her palm. Its rhythm contrasted sharply with the turmoil building beyond their sanctuary. "He's sowing discord and fear to weaken the bonds between our realms," she said, understanding dawning. "He uses the chaos he creates to justify further transgressions. It's twisted, but it would appeal to the darker elements of the Unseelie Court."

"Indeed," Kaelen agreed, his thumb tracing reassuring circles on her hand. "He spreads rumors that the Heartstone itself is destabilizing the Veil. That its awakening under your mortal care is a sign of impending doom rather than salvation. He tries to isolate you, to make you a pariah. And he paints me as a foolish prince who's been deceived by a mortal's charms."

Anger pricked at Elara's heart. To be branded as a danger when she had risked everything to protect the Heartstone, when she guarded it with her very life, cut deeply. Yet she could see the cruel effectiveness of Malakor's tactics. Fear and suspicion were powerful weapons.

"He wants to seize control before we can perform the Veil-mending ritual," she said, pieces falling into place. "He thrives on separation and discord. A healed Veil, realms working in harmony, would be antithetical to everything he represents."

"And he believes that by corrupting the Heartstone, he can prevent the ritual entirely," Kaelen added. "He imagines a world where the Unseelie dominate the mortal realm completely, where fear and shadow reign supreme. He underestimates the power of unity, of balance, and of the magic that's awakened in you."

Malakor's threat loomed large in their conversation, but here, within the protective embrace of the glade and bathed in the Heartstone's steady light, hope began to take root alongside the fear. His desperation was proof of the danger they posed to his plans. The race was on, and though the odds seemed overwhelming, Elara knew with absolute certainty that they would not falter.

They would recover their strength. They would plan their next moves carefully. And they would face the gathering darkness with a power as old as the realms themselves and as strong as the love that was blossoming between them.

The gentle luminescence of Eldoria's Cradle softened the edges of reality, creating a pocket of serenity where Malakor's storm felt distant, almost unreal. Yet both Elara and Kaelen knew the stillness was merely a prelude to the inevitable confrontation ahead.

Elara traced the delicate veins of a silver leaf between her fingers, its coolness a pleasant contrast to the warmth blooming in her chest whenever Kaelen's gaze met hers. They sat in shared silence for a long moment, both acutely aware of the monumental task that lay ahead and the personal cost it might demand.

"Malakor's desperation is palpable," Elara finally said, her voice low and thoughtful. "But I don't think he seeks power simply for its own sake. He wants to shatter the balance entirely, to sever the ancient ties between our realms permanently. He'll stop at nothing to achieve that vision."

She turned to look at Kaelen directly. "The path ahead is perilous. For both of us. For everyone we care about."

Kaelen shifted beside her, his presence a steady, comforting anchor in the uncertainty. He brushed her fingers where they rested on the Heartstone, the touch sending a familiar tremor of connection through both of them.

"The risks are immense," he acknowledged. "The Veil-mending ritual itself carries dangers that few truly understand. We're dealing with ancient forces, primal magics that existed before kingdoms or courts. If we fail, if we make even one mistake, the consequences could be catastrophic for both our realms."

He looked out over the tranquil glade, as if trying to fix its peaceful beauty in his memory before they had to leave it behind. "But I think the greater risk, the one that truly terrifies me, is the path we must walk together. You're mortal, Elara. I'm Unseelie Fae. Our worlds are divided by more than just a thin veil between dimensions. We're separated by centuries of distrust, by fundamental differences in our very natures."

His thumb traced slow, soothing circles on her hand, though even that gentle touch couldn't completely ease the knot of anxiety in her stomach. "And yet..." he continued softly.

"And yet," Elara whispered, finishing the thought, "it feels right. Being with you feels right in a way I can't fully explain."

She looked down at their joined hands. "I know your people view me with suspicion. I see it in their eyes when they think I'm not looking. Even among your allies, there are those who see me as a disruption, an outsider who doesn't belong in their world. And you're already walking a narrow ledge. Your defiance of Malakor's narrative hasn't gone unnoticed by the court."

A shadow crossed Kaelen's face. "Malakor exploits any deviation from the old order, any challenge to tradition. He calls our bond a betrayal of Fae purity. He rallies those who fear change, who cling to ancient prejudices. And there are moments when I fear the laws of my realm, the weight of centuries of tradition, could make him right in the eyes of many."

He paused, pain evident in his voice. "A union between a Fae prince and a mortal is not just rare or unusual, Elara. It's unheard of. It's condemned by many of the oldest laws. The consequences could be severe, not just for us, but for anyone who stands with us. I could lose my claim to the throne. I could be exiled. Or worse."

Elara's heart ached for him, for the impossible position he found himself in. She understood the weight of ancient law and tradition. But when she looked into his eyes, she saw beyond the prince to the man beneath, a man of unwavering kindness and fierce, protective resolve.

"Our connection feels deeper than politics or law," she said softly, her voice barely above a whisper. "When I'm with you, the world makes sense in a way it never did before. My magic sings in harmony with yours. The Heartstone responds to our combined will. It feels like we were meant to find each other, as if some force greater than either of us has been guiding our steps."

A rare, genuine smile touched Kaelen's lips, transforming his usually serious face. "And that is what terrifies me most," he admitted, his grip on her hand tightening. "This feeling has grown far beyond anything I expected or prepared for. It's like a forbidden bloom growing in barren land. I tried to deny it, tried to maintain proper distance. But I cannot. Not anymore."

He leaned closer, his voice dropping to a husky whisper that sent shivers down her spine. "Elara, my heart beats for you. I'm drawn to your strength, your resilience, the light that shines within you even in the darkest moments. You've seen the worst my realm has to offer, faced its shadows and dangers, and you don't flinch. Your courage, your compassion, they're intoxicating."

He searched her face, his expression a mixture of confession and plea. "This bond we share is more than just shared purpose or a convenient alliance. It's love. And I don't know what to do with that."

The word hung in the air between them, sacred and dangerous in equal measure. Elara's breath caught in her throat. She had dared to hope, had felt the same growing attachment, but hearing it spoken aloud, seeing it laid bare in his eyes, was both exhilarating and terrifying.

"I feel it too," she said, her voice trembling with the weight of truth. "This connection has wrapped itself around my soul like vines around an ancient tree. At first, I saw only a prince, a protector who offered hope against the blight. Now I see the man I love. Your faith in me, your willingness to defy your own people for what is right, these have captured my heart completely."

Tears shone in her eyes, though they were not born of sadness but of overwhelming, undeniable truth. "But I'm afraid of what this love means. For you, for me, for both our worlds. If Malakor can't break us through force, our own feelings might tear us apart. Can love truly cross such deep, ancient barriers? Or are we deluding ourselves?"

Kaelen brought her hand to his lips and kissed her knuckles with infinite tenderness. "I don't know," he said, his voice raw with honesty. "I can't promise you things I don't have the power to control. The path ahead is uncertain, and the cost may be higher than either of us can imagine. There are those in my court who would see us punished or even destroyed for this transgression. My claim to the throne, even my very life, could be forfeit."

His silver eyes burned with fierce resolve. "But I will not deny what I feel. I refuse to let fear dictate my heart. This love is not a weakness, Elara. It's the source of my strength. It fuels my fight against Malakor and his corruption. It guides me toward a vision of a brighter future, one where our realms can coexist in harmony rather than suspicion."

He cupped her face gently in his hands. "Whatever comes, whatever trials we must face, I want to face them with you. Together."

Elara leaned into his touch, letting the warmth of his hands chase away her fears, at least for this moment. "Together," she echoed, the word a vow and a prayer.

They sat in the glade's embrace as twilight deepened into night, holding each other close. The Heartstone pulsed between them, its light a gentle beacon in the darkness. Above, stars began to emerge, their ancient light bearing witness to a love that defied the boundaries of worlds.

Tomorrow would bring new challenges. Malakor's schemes would continue to unfold. The Veil would continue to weaken. But tonight, in Eldoria's Cradle, they had each other. And for now, that was enough.

Chapter 14

The morning after their confession brought no peace. The sky above Eldoria's Cradle had changed overnight, and not for the better. Where once there had been a consistent, gentle twilight, now there was chaos. A starlit sky warred against encroaching, unnatural darkness. It was as if the very boundaries of existence were fraying, threads of reality snapping under immense strain.

Kaelen stood by Elara's side at the edge of the glade, his usual stoicism edged with visible tension. His gaze was fixed on the pulsating distortion visible at the Veil's boundary, and his hand clasped hers tightly, a desperate anchor against the rising tide of chaos.

The magic within him, usually a controlled flame he could bank or release at will, now raged like a wild beast straining at its cage. It had been amplified by the Veil's instability, becoming dangerously unpredictable. He had tried throughout the night to bolster their defenses, to create a pocket of stability within the Cradle, but it was like trying to shore up a collapsing dam with bare hands.

"It's weakening at an alarming rate," he said, his voice low, barely audible above the Veil's agitated hum. "The curse, it's not just weakening the Veil anymore, Elara. It's tearing it from the inside out. And Malakor's power, amplified by this unrest, is becoming a destructive force unto itself."

Elara squeezed his hand, drawing what comfort she could from the contact. Her own magical reserves thrummed with nervous energy that felt both alien and terrifyingly familiar. The uncontrolled surges were becoming more frequent, more potent. It was as if the Veil's distress bled directly into her magic, amplifying its wildness and making it harder to control.

The Faewild's raw power churned around them, a tempest that threatened to overwhelm everything in its path.

"We need to perform the ritual," she said, her voice firm despite the despair closing in from all sides. "Now. We can't wait any longer for perfect conditions. The Veil is going to shatter if we don't act."

"Tomorrow," Kaelen agreed, though weariness clouded the usual luminescence of his silver eyes. "At the moon's zenith. It's the only time when the energies will be sufficiently aligned, even despite all this chaos."

His gaze swept across the violently swirling mist at the Veil's edge. "But the energies we'll be channeling won't be what we prepared for. They're infused with the curse's desperation now, with Malakor's dying rage. It will be a battle, Elara. A battle fought not just against external forces, but within ourselves. We'll have to maintain perfect control while channeling powers that want to tear us apart."

As if summoned by their very words, the air around them grew suddenly heavy, thick with an ancient, suffocating presence. The Cradle's protective glow dimmed, receding before a palpable aura of power rising at the glade's edge.

A figure stepped through the shimmering mist with unnerving grace that belied the oppressive power radiating from her form.

Lady Seraphina had returned.

Her presence jarred against the already discordant

atmosphere of the Faewild. She had been absent for weeks, her machinations cloaked in shadow and mystery. Now she stood before them, and her usual veiled amusement had been replaced by something far more dangerous: cold, absolute resolve.

Her eyes, which were often a deep, contemplative amethyst, now seemed to glow with an inner power that was almost painful to look at directly. The intricate silver embroidery of her flowing gown pulsed with a faint, ominous light that seemed to pulse in time with her heartbeat. She moved with the absolute authority of a queen returned to survey her fractured domain.

"You speak of a ritual," Seraphina said, her silken voice cutting through the agitated air like tempered steel. It resonated with depths that suggested ancient incantations and forgotten power. "A ritual to mend a veil that is already torn beyond recognition. How... quaint."

Kaelen stepped forward immediately, subtly placing himself between Seraphina and Elara. His posture became a silent challenge, his hand moving closer to his blade. "Lady Seraphina," he said, his voice carefully neutral though tension tightened every line of his shoulders. "Your presence is... unexpected."

A faint, cruel smile touched Seraphina's lips. "Is it? I would have thought my absence was the greater mystery, Lord Kaelen. But rest assured, I haven't been idle while you two toiled away in this tranquil little glade, playing at understanding forces beyond your comprehension. I have been weaving my own countermeasures, battling the encroaching chaos at its very source."

She gestured toward the trembling Veil with one elegant hand. "The curse's effects are far more insidious than either of you realize. They've seeped into the very fabric of magic itself, corrupting and twisting its essence at fundamental levels. Your attempt to 'mend' the Veil with your little ritual is like putting a bandage on a festering wound. It won't suffice. It can't suffice."

Elara watched her carefully, a knot of apprehension tightening in her stomach. Seraphina's certainty spoke of ancient knowledge, of secrets kept for millennia. But beneath that certainty lay something else: a hunger for control that sent shivers down Elara's spine.

"What have you been doing, Lady Seraphina?" Elara asked, keeping her voice steady despite her growing unease.

Seraphina's gaze shifted to Elara, and all traces of amusement vanished from her expression. "Reinforcing it, child," she said, her voice dropping to a conspiratorial whisper that somehow coiled around them despite the distance. "Not merely mending, but reweaving the Veil entirely. I have been imbuing it with my essence, with my power. Ancient magic that predates even this Cradle's founding. Magic that can truly stabilize, truly control the turbulent energies threatening to destroy both our worlds."

Kaelen's jaw tightened visibly. "You've been tampering with the Veil? Without our knowledge? Without consulting the Fae Council or seeking any kind of approval?"

She let out a soft, dismissive laugh that held no warmth. "The Fae Council? Those are merely shadows playing at governance while the world crumbles around them. Their methods are obsolete, their understanding of true power woefully inadequate. I, however, possess the knowledge to do what must be done. I have been preparing for this moment for centuries."

She stepped closer, and the air pressure seemed to thicken

with each step she took. "I know of your planned ritual. I know you think you can channel and contain this raw magic with your combined will and your precious Heartstone. You're fools, both of you. Your ritual will unleash a cataclysm, not provide a solution. You'll tear the Veil apart completely."

She stopped just a few feet away, her eyes locking first on Kaelen's, then flicking to Elara with an intensity that was almost physical. "Here is my proposal," she said, her voice taking on a resonant, almost hypnotic quality. "You will allow me to guide your ritual. My magic will be woven directly into yours. I will bind the Veil properly, not just mend it, but forge it anew into something stronger than it ever was before. I will ensure stability. I will ensure control. And I will ensure survival."

A chill crawled down Elara's spine. The way Seraphina spoke of "stability" and "control" carried unspoken threats. It sounded less like an offer of help and more like a promise of dominion.

"And if we refuse your generous offer?" Kaelen asked, his voice dangerously quiet, steady as a warrior bracing for inevitable battle.

Seraphina's smile returned, predatory and devoid of any warmth or genuine emotion. "Then I will act alone. The Veil is collapsing as we speak. If you won't help me harness its dying power properly, I will harness it myself. And if your ritual fails, or if I deem it insufficient to the task, I will tear down what little remains and rebuild the entire structure in my image. A realm governed by true strength, by true and absolute control."

She paused, letting the weight of her words settle over them. "The consequences for your mortal world, and even for the parts of the Faewild that still cling to your fragile, outdated ideals, will be... unpredictable. Likely devastating."

The implication was crystal clear. This was not an offer of partnership. This was a demand for surrender. She saw their ritual as clumsy and dangerous, and herself as the only true savior. Her power was undeniable, a force that had watched and waited in the shadows for who knew how long. Now she was demanding a seat at the very heart of their most crucial undertaking.

"You can't possibly believe your power alone can contain forces this ancient," Kaelen said, anger rising in his voice despite his attempts at control. "The Veil is meant to be a balance, not a weapon to be wielded."

"Balance is for the weak," Seraphina replied with obvious disdain. "Chaos is nature's true state, and order must be imposed upon it with an iron will. Your precious Veil is nothing but a suggestion of a barrier, a polite fiction. I will make it a fortress. An absolute wall between realms."

Her gaze pierced Elara with uncomfortable intensity. "And you, with your untamed mortal magic and your naive ideals, you are perhaps the most dangerous variable in all of this. You will not rebuild the Veil as a bridge between worlds. You will shatter it completely in your ignorance."

"You speak of control," Elara said, finding her voice and keeping it steady through sheer force of will. "But the Veil was always meant to be a bridge, not a prison. To rebuild it in your image, with your idea of 'control,' would sever the connection between realms entirely. That would lead to stagnation and eventual decay for both worlds."

"A sentimental notion," Seraphina sneered. "And one that will destroy everything you claim to hold dear. The Veil is failing. It is already becoming a chasm, not a bridge. My way ensures survival. Your way ensures oblivion for everyone."

She stepped even closer, her voice dropping to something low and intense. "The ritual will proceed tomorrow, as you have planned. But it will proceed with my guidance, with my magic woven into the very foundations of what you build. You will incorporate my methods, my power. If you cooperate, we might achieve true stability. But if you resist..."

She let the threat hang in the air between them, unfinished but absolutely clear.

"I will shatter what little remains of the Veil myself and forge my own path forward. The consequences will be severe for everyone. But at least there will be order. At least there will be survival, even if not everyone survives to see it."

Silence crackled between them like lightning waiting to strike. Seraphina's ultimatum offered a cruel choice: accept help from someone who clearly sought dominion rather than balance, or risk both the Veil's complete collapse and her direct, hostile intervention.

Kaelen held her gaze, his jaw set in determination. He could feel the immensity of her power radiating from her like heat from a forge. It rivaled his own considerable abilities, perhaps even surpassed them in raw, ancient fury. To include her in their ritual would be to invite a serpent into their sanctuary, to give her access to the very heart of what they were trying to build.

Yet the alternative, total collapse followed by Seraphina reshaping reality according to her own dark vision, was equally terrifying.

"You underestimate us," Kaelen finally said, his natural authority returning despite his weariness. "We have worked tirelessly to understand the Veil's nature. We have prepared for this ritual with everything we have. We know the risks we're taking, and we will face them on our own terms."

"Prepared?" Seraphina scoffed, genuine derision in her voice. "You are children playing with fire you don't understand. Malakor's curse is merely a symptom, not the disease. The Veil has always been fragile, always been a flawed creation from its inception. I will rectify that fundamental flaw."

She tilted her head, her eyes gleaming with something almost like pity. "Consider this your only real chance at survival. The ritual proceeds tomorrow at moonrise, whether you cooperate or not. Whether it becomes a shared undertaking or mine alone remains to be seen. But make no mistake: the Veil will be reforged, one way or another. The only question is whether you'll be part of the solution or swept aside with the problem."

With that ominous declaration, Seraphina turned with fluid grace. Her silken gown swirled around her like a living shadow, like a dark omen given physical form. She glided toward the Veil's chaotic edge, her form beginning to dissolve into the mist as mysteriously as she had arrived.

But even after she vanished completely, the air still vibrated with the echo of her power. It was a chilling reminder of the adversary they now faced, someone who might be even more dangerous than Malakor in her own way.

Elara looked at Kaelen, her heart heavy with the weight of impossible choices. The Veil's tremors seemed to mock their predicament, growing stronger with each passing moment. They were caught between a collapsing world and the machinations of a power-hungry sorceress who saw them as obstacles to be removed or tools to be used.

Could they trust the viper in their midst? Or would refusal

guarantee their destruction at her hands?

The night stretched before them, a dark canvas on which the fate of two worlds would soon be painted. A tapestry woven with desperation, power, and the chilling ambiguity of Seraphina's true intentions.

The weight of the decision settled on both their shoulders, heavier than any magic either had ever wielded.

Tomorrow, everything would change.

Chapter 15

The moon rose over the Whispering Falls, full and heavy in the sky, casting silver light across the sacred ground where Elara and Kaelen had chosen to perform the ritual. The Falls themselves cascaded down ancient stone, their mist creating rainbows in the moonlight that seemed almost magical in their own right.

This was it. The moment everything had been building toward.

Elara stood at the center of a carefully drawn circle, the Heartstone pulsing in her hands. Around her, Kaelen had placed markers at each cardinal point: earth from the Heartwood Grove, water from the purest spring, fire contained in enchanted crystal, and air represented by wind chimes that sang in the breeze.

"Are you ready?" Kaelen asked, taking his position opposite her in the circle.

Elara met his eyes across the space. "As ready as I'll ever be."

The Veil above them was visible now, shimmering and torn in places, barely holding together. Every moment they delayed brought it closer to complete collapse. But rushing would be just as dangerous. This ritual required perfect balance, perfect focus.

"Then let us begin," Kaelen said.

He began to chant in the ancient Fae tongue, words that

predated kingdoms and courts, words of pure magic. Elara joined him, speaking the counterpoint she had learned from the spirits, her mortal voice blending with his Fae melody.

The Heartstone began to glow brighter, responding to their combined will.

Power surged through the circle, drawn from the elements around them. Elara felt it flowing into her, through her, amplified by the Heartstone she held. It was intoxicating and terrifying in equal measure. So much power. More than she had ever wielded before.

The Veil responded. The tears began to pulse, as if the fabric of reality itself was breathing.

"Focus on the largest tear," Kaelen instructed, his voice strained with the effort of channeling so much magic. "We'll work our way to the smaller ones."

Elara directed her attention to a massive rent in the Veil, a wound that leaked corrupted energy like blood from a mortal wound. She reached out with her magic, guided by the Heartstone, and began to weave.

It was like sewing, but instead of thread, she used strands of pure light and shadow, mortal resilience and Fae grace. Each stitch pulled at her strength, draining her reserves, but she could see it working. The tear was closing.

"From the heart of the earth, the breath of the wind," she chanted, pouring her will into the words, "from the light of the sun, the depth of the sea. I call forth the essence of life. Let this wound be healed. Let this tear be sealed. Let the tapestry be whole again."

The Heartstone flared with brilliant golden light. A torrent of energy surged outward, guided by her hands and amplified by her intent. The light struck the torn Veil, and the darkness that had been seeping through recoiled as if burned.

The frayed edges began to knit together, slowly but irrevocably.

The mental strain was immense. She had to keep her mind perfectly still, perfectly focused, in the middle of a torrent of raw power. Any lapse in concentration could cause the threads to snap, undoing all her work and possibly tearing the Veil apart completely.

Fatigue pressed in from all sides, a crushing weight that threatened to overwhelm her. But the sight of the Veil beginning to heal, the shimmer returning to its surface, drove her onward.

Kaelen's magic flowed around her like a protective cocoon, supporting her, lending his strength when hers wavered. "You are strong," he murmured, his voice reaching her even through the roar of power. "Stronger than you know. Trust your instincts. Trust the magic. Trust yourself."

His words soothed her fraying spirit, gave her the strength to continue. She turned her attention to another wound in the Veil, this one crackling with unstable energy, a severed connection that was letting wild magic spill through in chaotic bursts.

Her hands moved with growing confidence, weaving threads of controlled power to replace the broken ones.

"As the river is guided by its banks," she chanted, her voice growing more sure with each word, "so shall this energy find its course. Not contained, but harmonized. Let balance be restored."

The volatile energy responded to her touch, its frantic

crackling subsiding as her carefully woven threads integrated into the Veil's fabric. The shimmer pulsed, growing steadier, as the chaos found its channel and flowed smoothly once more.

The toll on her body was immense. Every fiber of her being felt stretched thin, like cloth pulled to its breaking point. But the results were tangible, undeniable. The Veil, though still scarred, was growing whole again, its shimmer brighter and more stable with each passing moment.

With a deep, steadying breath, Elara turned to face the largest tear of all. This was the wound where Malakor's malice had festered, where corruption had eaten deepest into the Veil's fabric. Dark energy pulsed from it like a diseased heartbeat.

She held the Heartstone high, feeling its dual energies, mortal and Fae, resonating with her intent. The stone seemed to understand what was needed. It pulsed in time with her own heartbeat, linking them together.

She began to chant, and this time the words of renewal rang through the glen with power that shook the very air.

"From the heart of the earth, the breath of the wind, the light of the sun, the depth of the sea," she intoned, each word carrying the weight of absolute conviction. "I call forth the essence of life itself. Let this wound be purged of darkness. Let corruption be banished. Let the tapestry be whole, vibrant, and unbroken once more."

She poured her very essence into the Heartstone, everything she had left, amplified by the sacred ground's power and by Kaelen's unwavering support. Golden light erupted from the stone, warm and life-affirming, bathing the torn Veil in cleansing radiance that seemed to carry the promise of dawn after the longest night.

The darkness recoiled from that light like a living thing

fleeing pain.

Sharp, lancing pain tore through Elara, proof of the tremendous energy she was channeling. Her vision swam, the world tilting dangerously. Her knees buckled, but Kaelen was there instantly, his steadying hand on her shoulder, his magic supporting hers, keeping her anchored to reality.

Slowly, so slowly it seemed to take an eternity, the massive tear's edges began to knit together. Golden light permeated the wound, purifying and healing. The Veil hummed with what could only be described as relief, like a wounded creature finally finding comfort.

The destructive, corrupted energy that had poisoned this place for so long dissipated, replaced by a gentle, vibrant pulse of healthy magic.

The process had drained Elara to her very core. She had nothing left to give. Yet when the final stitch sealed that terrible wound, when she saw the Veil whole once more, peace washed over her in a wave so powerful it brought tears to her eyes.

The Veil still bore its marks, the scars of what it had endured. But it was no longer broken. Its integrity had returned.

Then the air, thick with nascent magic and the smell of rain and earth, shattered.

A violent rupture tore through their fragile peace. The sky, which had been soft twilight just moments before, erupted in dark, roiling energy. Thunder crashed without clouds. Lightning forked across the heavens in patterns that defied nature.

Malakor had arrived, and he had not come alone.

From jagged tears in space itself, shadow-wrought soldiers

poured forth. Behind them moved darker figures, lieutenants whose very presence radiated malice and corruption. And at their center stood Malakor himself, a figure of obsidian and burning ambition, his eyes twin embers of hatred fixed directly on Elara.

"Foolish mortals and fickle Fae," Malakor's voice boomed across the Falls, carrying power that shook the stones themselves. "Did you truly believe you could mend what I have broken? Your petty rituals cannot defy the inevitable march of destiny."

Beside her, Kaelen moved with the deadly speed of a striking viper. His Fae blade, usually a mere whisper of silver, now blazed with defiant light that seemed to challenge the very darkness Malakor commanded. He set his stance between Elara and the approaching army, a bulwark of unwavering power and absolute determination.

"You are not welcome here," Kaelen growled, his voice carrying all the authority of his royal blood. "This place is sacred. You defile it with your presence."

Malakor's laugh was humorless and cold as winter's deepest night. "Sacred? This place will bear my mark before this night is through. And you, dear brother, will be the first to fall. Your resistance has always been so... predictable."

With a casual flick of his wrist, Malakor unleashed a torrent of living shadow. Kaelen met it head-on, his blade carving a path through the darkness. The impact sent a shockwave through the glen that made the trees bend and the stones crack. Leaves and debris flew in all directions.

The shadow soldiers surged forward like a dark tide. Kaelen became a whirlwind of silver and light, his blade a blur as he met their advance. Each stroke was precise, economical, deadly.

Soldiers fell, dissolving into acrid smoke, but more kept coming.

Caught between the desperate need to complete the ritual and the chaos of battle erupting around her, Elara felt her grip on the magic waver. The Heartstone's warmth turned suddenly cold in her hands. The carefully woven threads she had created began to fray at the edges.

The balance she had fought so hard to restore teetered on the edge of collapse.

"Focus, Elara!" Kaelen's voice cut through the din of battle, sharp and clear. "Do not let his chaos break your will. You are the Weaver. The Veil needs you now more than ever."

His words were a lifeline thrown across stormy waters. She forced her eyes away from the battle, back to the shimmering expanse of the Veil above. The raw magic of this sacred place swirled around her, volatile now, responding to the violence and fear.

She anchored herself to the Heartstone's pulse and to Kaelen's steadfast defense. Her trembling hands moved to reweave the damaged strands, to shore up what Malakor's arrival had threatened to undo.

One of Malakor's lieutenants, a hulking brute with armor of shadow-forged steel, broke through Kaelen's defense. It lunged directly for Elara, its obsidian mace swinging in a deadly arc aimed at the Heartstone itself.

Time seemed to stretch, every second lasting an eternity. Kaelen was too far away, engaged with three other attackers. He couldn't possibly intercept in time.

Instinct took over. Elara dropped the Heartstone and threw herself aside. The mace struck the ground where she had been standing just a heartbeat before, sending stone shards flying like shrapnel. One cut her cheek, drawing blood.

Before the lieutenant could recover for another strike, Kaelen was there. He had broken away from his other opponents with impossible speed. His blade, blazing with fury and desperation, sliced through the creature's armor as if it were made of paper. It dissolved into acrid, choking smoke.

"Are you hurt?" Kaelen's voice was ragged, his breathing labored.

Elara shook her head, gasping for air. "No. But the Heartstone..."

She looked down in horror. The Heartstone lay on the ground, exposed and vulnerable, its light flickering uncertainly.

Malakor saw it. His eyes lit up with predatory delight.

"Seize it," he commanded his remaining forces.

The soldiers surged toward the Heartstone like moths to flame. Kaelen roared and tried to break free to defend it, but for every foe he cut down, two more rose from the churning darkness to take its place.

Elara's heart hammered in her chest. She could feel the ritual faltering, feel the Veil beginning to tear again, wider and more violent than before. The sacred ground's power was becoming a raging torrent, too chaotic to channel, too wild to control.

"Kaelen, I can't maintain it," she cried out, desperation bleeding into her voice. "The ritual is breaking apart. The Veil is tearing again!"

Kaelen fought harder, his blade becoming a desperate dance of light and fury. "Hold on, Elara. The power of this place and the strength of your lineage are within you. You are more than you know. Fight!"

His words struck something deep within her. She remembered the spirits' teachings, the Heartwood's wisdom. She was not just a conduit for power. She was a bridge between worlds. That was her true strength.

She looked at the Heartstone where it lay, its surface reflecting the chaos swirling around them. And in that reflection, she saw truth.

Sensing her moment of wavering, Malakor raised his hand high. A sphere of dark energy formed above his palm, crackling with malevolent power, pulsing with destructive intent. It grew larger, feeding on the ambient fear and violence.

He aimed it directly at the Heartstone.

"This ends now," he hissed, triumph dripping from every word.

Elara's eyes widened in horror. If that orb struck the Heartstone, it would shatter the artifact into a thousand pieces. And with it would die any hope of healing the Veil.

With a primal cry that came from the deepest part of her soul, Elara lunged forward. She dove toward the Heartstone, making her own body a barrier between it and annihilation.

Kaelen saw her move. His roar of alarm echoed across the Falls, raw and agonized. But even as the sound left his lips, he understood what she was doing. And he knew what he had to do.

As Elara's fingers brushed the Heartstone's surface, Malakor released the orb of destruction. It hurtled through the air like a falling star, trailing darkness in its wake.

At the last possible instant, Kaelen threw himself between Elara and certain death. His blade flared with every ounce of power he possessed, transforming into a shield, a dome of incandescent Fae energy that blazed like a second sun.

The orb struck with the force of a collapsing star.

Light and shadow exploded outward in a catastrophic burst. The shield buckled under the assault, cracks spreading across its surface like lightning. Then it shattered completely, raining down in fragments of dying light.

The force of the explosion hurled Kaelen backward. He slammed against the ancient stones with bone-crushing impact. His blade clattered from his grasp and went dark, its light extinguished. He lay utterly still.

Malakor's laughter echoed across the battlefield, cold and triumphant. "The guardian falls. Now the little mender has no one left to protect her."

He began to advance, his eyes burning with the promise of victory.

Elara knelt beside Kaelen, her breath catching in her throat. His chest rose and fell in shallow, irregular gasps. His vibrant magic, which had always burned so bright, had dimmed to the barest flicker. He had taken the full force of that blast to save her and the Heartstone.

Tears streamed down her face, hot and bitter. The ritual, all their hope, it all felt so fragile now. So impossibly distant.

As her tears fell on Kaelen's still form, something shifted. A faint pulse of Fae magic responded to her touch, to her sorrow and love. It was tiny, barely there, but present. And with it came the Heartwood's whisper, as clear as if the ancient trees stood beside her:

Even in the deepest darkness, life finds a way.

Malakor's shadow fell over her, blotting out the moon. "It is over, little Weaver. Your champion has fallen. Your ritual has failed. And now you will watch as I tear down everything you tried to build."

Elara looked up at him. Grief clouded her vision, but beneath it, something else stirred. Something vast and ancient and furious.

She remembered her grandmother's words, spoken so long ago: *Duality is not weakness but the source of true strength.*

She was both mortal and Fae-touched. Both grounded and wild. Both order and chaos. Not one or the other, but both at once. That was her power. That was what made her unique.

The raw power of the nexus swirled around her, responding to her rising determination. It no longer felt foreign or frightening. It felt like coming home.

"You're wrong," she said, her voice quiet but carrying absolute conviction. "This isn't over. It's only beginning."

She placed one hand on Kaelen's chest, feeling the faint flutter of his heartbeat. With the other, she grasped the Heartstone. And she opened herself fully to the power of this sacred place, no longer trying to control or direct it, but inviting it in. Welcoming it.

The transformation was instantaneous.

Power flooded into her in a torrent, mortal and Fae, order and chaos, light and shadow, all flowing together in perfect harmony. The Heartstone blazed in her hand, brighter than it had ever shone before.

Malakor stumbled back, genuine surprise crossing his

features. "What... what are you?"

"I am the bridge," Elara said, and her voice carried the echo of wind through ancient forests and the crash of waves on distant shores. "I am the Weaver. And you will not break what I have woven."

She stood, and power rippled outward from her in waves. The threads of the Veil responded to her call, strengthening, intertwining. Where before she had carefully stitched each tear, now the Veil began to heal itself, guided by her will but empowered by something far greater.

Malakor snarled and threw another bolt of dark energy at her. She didn't dodge. She didn't need to. The power simply dissipated when it touched her, absorbed and transformed into light.

"Impossible," Malakor breathed.

"You seek to control," Elara said, advancing on him step by step. "But true power lies in understanding. In harmony. In balance. You have none of these things. And so you will fall."

She raised the Heartstone high, and its light exploded outward, a wave of pure, cleansing energy that swept across the battlefield. Malakor's shadow soldiers dissolved like mist before the sun. His lieutenants fell, their corrupted forms unable to withstand such purity.

Malakor himself staggered, his power wavering. "No... I am darkness eternal. I cannot be defeated by mere light."

"You're not eternal," Elara said softly. "You're just afraid. Afraid of change. Afraid of losing control. Afraid of being insignificant." She looked at him with something almost like pity. "But your fear ends here."

She channeled the full power of the Heartstone through herself and into the Veil. Golden light erupted like a new dawn, washing over everything. The last tears in the Veil sealed shut. The corruption that had plagued it for so long burned away. And the balance, the perfect equilibrium between order and chaos, snapped into place.

Malakor screamed as the light touched him. His form began to dissolve, his stolen power unraveling. "This isn't over," he hissed even as he faded. "I will return. Darkness always returns."

"And light will always rise to meet it," Elara said. "But you? You're done."

With a final, agonized cry, Malakor dissolved completely, leaving nothing behind but fading shadows.

Elara stood in the sudden silence, breathing hard. The Veil above her shimmered with renewed strength, whole and healthy. The ritual was complete. They had won.

Then she remembered Kaelen.

She dropped to her knees beside him, setting the Heartstone aside. "Kaelen. Kaelen, please. Wake up."

His eyes flickered open slowly. "Elara?" His voice was barely a whisper.

"I'm here," she said, tears flowing freely now. "You saved me. You idiot, you could have died."

"Worth it," he managed, a ghost of his usual smile touching his lips. "Did we... did you..."

"It's done," she said. "The Veil is healed. Malakor is gone. We won."

"We?" he asked. "Sounds like... you did most of it."

"We," she insisted. "I couldn't have done any of it without you."

She placed her hands on his chest, and drew on the last reserves of her power. She channeled healing energy into him, using everything the Heartstone and the sacred ground could give her. Slowly, agonizingly slowly, color returned to his face. His breathing steadied.

After what felt like hours but was probably only minutes, Kaelen sat up, still weak but alive.

"That was..." he began.

"Terrifying?" Elara suggested.

"I was going to say incredible," he said, taking her hand. "You were incredible."

She helped him to his feet, and together they looked up at the healed Veil, shimmering and strong above them.

"We did it," Kaelen said softly. "We actually did it."

"We did," Elara agreed. "And now..."

"Now," Kaelen said, turning to face her, "now we build something better. Together."

He pulled her into his arms, and she went willingly, burying her face against his chest. They had survived. Against all odds, against impossible forces, they had survived. And they had saved both their worlds.

As dawn broke over the Whispering Falls, painting the sky in shades of rose and gold, Elara and Kaelen stood together at the edge of a new era. The thorns of the past had given way to the promise of a future bright with possibility.

And they would face that future the way they had faced everything else.

Together.

Epilogue

Six Months Later

The forest no longer whispered warnings. It sang.

Dawn poured through the canopy like liquid gold, pooling at Elara's feet as she stood before the Veil, in the place where worlds had once collided and bled. The air shimmered softly here, no longer a wound in reality but a living breath between realms, a gentle boundary that welcomed crossing rather than forbidding it.

She reached out, her fingertips brushing the invisible current, and it thrummed in answer. Not in hunger or desperation, but in recognition. She had feared this resonance once, had been terrified of the power that connected her to this liminal space. Now it was as natural as breathing, as fundamental as her own heartbeat.

Six months had passed since the ritual at the Whispering Falls. Six months since Malakor's defeat and the Veil's healing. In that time, the world had transformed in ways both subtle and profound.

Oakhaven had returned to its quiet rhythm, but with new additions. Children's laughter still drifted from the village green, but now Fae children played alongside mortal ones, their pointed ears and luminous eyes no longer objects of fear but of wonder. The scent of lavender from Maeve's garden still lingered in the breeze, and her grandmother was stronger now, her illness fading as the blight's influence lifted from the land.

"You still come here every morning," a familiar voice said behind her.

Elara smiled without turning. She knew that voice as well as her own. "It calls to me," she said simply. "The Veil. It speaks in a language I'm only just beginning to understand."

Kaelen stepped from the dappled shadows, his silver eyes softer than they had been six months ago. The weight of his curse, the burden he'd carried for so long, had lifted completely. Shadows and sunlight played across his face in equal measure, neither dominating, both in perfect balance.

He had changed in the months since their victory. The hard edges of the warrior prince had softened, replaced by something more thoughtful, more at peace. He no longer wore his armor constantly, and his hand rarely strayed to his sword. The need for such constant vigilance had passed.

"It listens as well," Kaelen murmured, moving to stand beside her. He gazed at the Veil with something like affection. "I can feel it when I'm near. It remembers what we did. What you did."

Elara shook her head gently. "What we did together. I couldn't have healed it alone."

"Perhaps," Kaelen conceded. He reached for her hand, no longer in desperation or fear, but in simple affection and reverence. Their fingers intertwined, mortal and Fae, the space between them alive with quiet magic that was neither his nor hers but theirs together.

"The Veil may be mended," he said softly, "but its scars remain. Like us."

Elara looked down at their joined hands. She still bore a thin silver scar on her palm from the ritual, a mark that would never fade. Kaelen had similar scars across his chest from Malakor's attack, though Fae healing had rendered them almost invisible. But she knew they were there, just as he knew about hers.

"Scars are proof we survived," she whispered. "They're proof we fought for something worth fighting for."

A breeze rippled through the clearing, carrying the faint, haunting hum of the Veil. Not a warning this time, but a greeting. A promise.

Kaelen turned to face her fully, his expression serious. "There's something I need to tell you. The Council convenes tomorrow in Eldoria. Both councils, actually. Seelie and Unseelie together for the first time in centuries."

Elara's eyebrows rose. "Together? In the same room?"

"In the same city," Kaelen corrected with a slight smile. "We're taking small steps. But yes, there will be representatives from both courts, and from the mortal kingdoms as well. It's unprecedented."

"What will they discuss?"

"Us," Kaelen said simply. "Our bond. What it means for the future of both realms. And..." He paused, seeming to gather his courage. "There are those who wish to formalize our union. To make it official in the eyes of both Fae and mortal law."

Elara's heart skipped a beat. "Marriage?"

"More than marriage," Kaelen said. "A binding. A covenant between realms. You would be recognized as my equal, not as a consort but as a co-ruler. The first mortal to hold such a position in Fae history."

The implications took Elara's breath away. She had known their relationship was significant, had understood that it symbolized the new connection between their worlds. But this was something else entirely.

"That's... that's enormous," she managed. "There will be opposition. From both sides."

"Undoubtedly," Kaelen agreed. "There are still those in my court who view mortals as lesser, who believe the old ways should be maintained. And there are mortals who fear the Fae, who see this as some kind of takeover or corruption of mortal sovereignty."

"Are they wrong to be concerned?" Elara asked quietly.

Kaelen met her eyes steadily. "I cannot promise that this path will be easy. I cannot guarantee that everyone will accept what we're building. But I can promise that I will stand beside you, that I will fight for this vision of a united future. And I can promise that my love for you is not politics or strategy. It's real, Elara. It's the most real thing I've ever known."

Tears pricked at Elara's eyes, but they were tears of joy rather than sorrow. "I love you too," she said. "And I want this. I want to build this new world with you. But..."

"But?" Kaelen prompted gently.

"But I'm afraid," Elara admitted. "I'm afraid of failing. I'm afraid of not being enough. I'm a village herbalist, Kaelen. Six months ago, I was tending gardens and mixing tinctures. Now people are talking about making me a queen. How can I possibly be ready for that?"

Kaelen brought her hand to his lips, pressing a kiss to her scarred palm. "You stood against Malakor and won. You healed a wound in reality itself. You wielded power that would have destroyed most beings and used it to create rather than destroy. If that doesn't qualify you to lead, nothing does."

"You make it sound so simple," Elara said with a weak laugh.

"It's not simple at all," Kaelen said honestly. "It will be the hardest thing either of us has ever done. Building a new world is always harder than maintaining an old one. But we won't be alone. We have allies. We have people who believe in this vision."

He gestured back toward the forest path, where figures were beginning to emerge in the early morning light. Elara recognized them: Lady Moraine of the Seelie Court, her stern features softened by cautious optimism. Captain Theron from the mortal guard, who had fought beside them against Malakor's forces. Even a few former members of the Unseelie Court who had turned against Malakor in the final days.

And there, walking with surprising steadiness, was Maeve. Her grandmother smiled at her across the distance, pride shining in her eyes.

"They've come for the announcement," Kaelen said quietly. "If you're ready. If you choose this path."

Elara looked at the gathered crowd, then at the Veil shimmering peacefully behind her, then finally at Kaelen's face. She saw hope there, and love, and determination.

"I choose this," she said firmly. "I choose us. I choose this future we're building together."

Kaelen's smile was radiant. He raised their joined hands high, and a cheer went up from the gathered witnesses. It was a small crowd, nothing like the massive assemblies that would come later. But it was a beginning.

Lady Moraine stepped forward, her expression formal but not unkind. "Then let it be known," she said, her voice carrying with Fae magic, "that Elara of Oakhaven and Prince Kaelen of the Unseelie Court are recognized as bound by the ancient rites. Let their union stand as a bridge between our peoples, as a symbol of the new age we are entering together."

The formal words echoed across the clearing, sealing something that had already been true in Elara's heart for months.

As the witnesses approached to offer congratulations and blessings, Elara felt a strange pull at the edges of her awareness. She turned back to the Veil, frowning slightly.

"What is it?" Kaelen asked, noticing her distraction.

"I don't know," Elara said slowly. "Something feels... different. The Veil is trying to tell me something."

She focused her attention fully on the shimmering boundary, opening her senses the way she had learned to do during the ritual. The Veil's song changed pitch, becoming more urgent. Images began to form in her mind, hazy and incomplete.

Darkness. But not Malakor's darkness. Something older. Something that had been sleeping, and was now beginning to wake.

A figure cloaked in starlight and shadow, neither fully Fae nor mortal but something else entirely. Ancient eyes that held the weight of millennia. A voice that whispered of debts unpaid and balances that must be restored.

"The healing of the Veil," the vision seemed to say, "has consequences. You have restored what was broken, but in doing so, you have awakened what was meant to remain sleeping. The Reckoning approaches."

The images faded, leaving Elara gasping slightly.

"Elara?" Kaelen's voice was sharp with concern. "What did you see?"

"I'm not sure," Elara said honestly. She looked up at him, seeing the worry in his eyes. "But I think... I think our work isn't finished. The Veil is healed, yes. But healing it may have triggered something else. Something we didn't anticipate."

Kaelen's expression grew serious, but not frightened. "Then we'll face it," he said simply. "Whatever comes next, we'll face it together. That's what we do."

Elara nodded, drawing strength from his certainty. He was right. They had faced impossible odds before and prevailed. Whatever this new challenge might be, they would meet it the same way.

But not today. Today was for celebration, for hope, for the beginning of something beautiful and new.

She turned back to their gathered friends and allies, pushing her concerns about the vision to the back of her mind. There would be time to investigate, to prepare, to understand what the Veil's warning meant.

For now, she simply took Kaelen's hand and walked back toward the people who believed in them, toward the future they were building together.

The sun rose higher, painting the sky in shades of rose and gold. The Veil shimmered peacefully at their backs, a bridge between worlds, a promise of possibility. And though darkness might be stirring somewhere in the depths, today was filled with light.

Elara smiled as Maeve embraced her, as Lady Moraine offered a rare smile, as Captain Theron clapped Kaelen on the shoulder with genuine affection. This was what they had fought for. Not just the healing of the Veil, but this: connection, community, hope.

As they walked back toward Oakhaven together, leaving the Veil to its peaceful vigil, Elara felt the weight of destiny settling on her shoulders. But it didn't feel burdensome. It felt right.

She was no longer just a village herbalist. She was a Weaver, a bridge, a queen in waiting. And beside her walked a prince who had become so much more: partner, protector, love.

Whatever challenges lay ahead, whatever darkness the Veil's warning spoke of, they would face it together. They had saved two worlds once.

If necessary, they would do it again.

But for today, for this perfect morning filled with golden light and the laughter of friends, they simply walked hand in hand toward home.

The story of Elara and Kaelen was far from over. In many ways, it was only beginning.

But that was a tale for another day.

The Veil stood silent and strong, a testament to courage, love, and the power of unity. And in its depths, ancient forces began to stir, preparing for the reckoning yet to come.

End of Book One

Map Of Eldoria
And The Faewild

The Known Realms of Eldoria

- **Oakhaven** – A quiet village cradled by rolling hills and ancient oaks. Known for its herbalists and whispered legends of the Veil.

- **The Whispering Woods** – A vast forest where the mortal world thins and the boundary of the Veil hums like a living heart.

- **Silvermere Lake** – Said to mirror the moonlight of both realms. Some claim its depths touch the Faewild's rivers of starlight.

- **The Wyrdstones** – Standing stones older than history, each etched with runes that shimmer faintly beneath new moons.

- **The Frosted Peaks** – Northern mountains said to conceal portals that flicker open during storms.

The Faewild Beyond the Veil

- **The Unseelie Court of Dusk** – Kaelen's realm, a kingdom of twilight and sorrow where beauty walks hand in hand with ruin.

- **The Seelie Court of Dawn** – Their radiant rivals, sworn to preserve order through light — though their grace hides its own cruelty.

- **The Shadowgroves** – Living forests where trees whisper in voices older than the stars.

- **The River Lirion** – A silver current flowing through both realms, said to remember every promise ever spoken.

- **The Hollow Citadel** – A forgotten stronghold lost between light and dark, rumored to be where the Veil first tore.

MAP OF ELDORIA
AND THE FAEWILD
THE UNSEELIE
COURT OF DUSK
THE SEELIE
COURT OF DAWN
THE VEIL
THE
SHADOWGROVES
TH HOLLOW
CITADEL
OAKHAVEN
THE FROSTED
PEAKS
THE KNOWN
REALMS OF ELDORIA

Glossary
Dramatis Personae

Key Terms

- **The Veil** – The shimmering barrier dividing the mortal world (Eldoria) from the Faewild. It is not a wall, but a living weave of magic and will.

- **The Veilbound** – Those rare souls attuned to the Veil's song, capable of sensing or crossing between realms.

- **Resonance** – The echoing vibration felt by those connected to the Veil's energy; a sign of awakening power.

- **Heartstone** – A conduit of pure Veil energy, capable of amplifying or mending rifts between worlds.

- **Unseelie / Seelie** – The twin courts of the Faewild. The Unseelie embody dusk, decay, and truth through chaos; the Seelie embody dawn, creation, and control through order.

- **The Weave** – The living threads of existence linking every realm, emotion, and destiny.

Principal Characters

- **Elara of Oakhaven** – A healer with an intuitive bond to the natural world. Her quiet life is forever altered when she touches the Veil and draws the attention of the Fae.

- **Kaelen, Prince of the Unseelie Fae** – A cursed immortal whose bloodline decays under the weight of a broken ancient pact. Bound by desperation and honor, he seeks Elara's aid to restore balance.

- **Maeve** – Elara's grandmother and mentor, keeper of forgotten lore and living memory of the old ways.

- **The Veil Itself** – Neither good nor evil. It is the consciousness between realms, watching, yearning, and whispering to those who listen.

- **Malakor** – A ruthless and ambitious member of the Unseelie Court who seeks to control the Veil and seize power for himself. His dark machinations and hunger for dominance drive the story's central conflict.

- **Seraphina** – An ancient sorceress of uncertain allegiance who offers Elara guidance and power, though her true motivations remain shrouded in mystery and her aid comes at a dangerous price.

- **Moraine** – An Elder of the Seelie Court whose stern wisdom and pragmatic approach play a crucial role in navigating the political tensions between the courts.

Acknowledgements

To the dreamers who walk the edge of the Veil, this story was written for you.

To every reader who believes that love can be both a weapon and a healing touch, thank you for lending your heart to this world. You breathed life into its shadows and gave meaning to its light.

To the friends, family, and quiet believers who reminded me to keep going, your patience and faith carried me through every storm. You are the unseen hands behind every page.

To the storytellers who came before me, whose words taught me that magic lives in the spaces between sorrow and hope, this book stands because of you.

And to those who have ever felt too wild, too soft, or too much: may you never dull your light to fit a dim world. You are proof that the broken can still bloom, and that even the smallest spark can set the dark alight.

With endless love and gratitude,

Eira Blackthorn

Reading Group 3 Reflection Questions

1. Elara often struggles between her mortal heart and her connection to the Veil.

   How does this duality mirror the balance between light and shadow throughout the story?

2. Kaelen's power is both a curse and a duty.

   What does his journey reveal about the price of leadership and the vulnerability of love?

3. The Veil is both barrier and bridge — a symbol of separation, yet also connection.

   How does this reflect Elara and Kaelen's relationship?

4. Elara learns that compassion can be a form of strength.

   Do you believe empathy can coexist with power in a world built on control and fear?

5. Several characters wrestle with destiny versus choice.

   Which moments in the story show the consequences of choosing one over the other?

6. Magic in *Thorns of the Veil* is closely tied to emotion and memory. What does this suggest about the true

nature of magic, and how might that evolve in the next book?

7. If you could step through the Veil for a single day, where would you go, the mortal realm or the Faewild, and why?

Series Overview
The Veilbound Saga

Book One – *Thorns of the Veil*

A healer's touch awakens the boundary between realms, and the heart of a cursed Fae prince. Love blossoms where shadow meets light, and the Veil demands its due.

Book Two – *Embers of the Veil*

Peace is a fragile illusion. When whispers rise from beneath the ash and the Fae courts fracture, Elara and Kaelen must face a truth darker than prophecy: some wounds burn long after the Veil has healed.

Book Three – *Crown of Ash and Starlight*

The balance falters, the bond deepens, and the realms tremble as the fire beneath the Veil begins to consume everything it once protected.

Book Four – *The Shattered Veil*

The saga concludes where it began, in light, in shadow, and in the unbreakable thread between two hearts bound by fate.

Sneak Preview
Coming Soon
Book Two of The Veilbound Saga

Embers of the Veil

The balance Elara fought to weave has begun to unravel.

Beneath the roots of Eldoria, something ancient stirs older than the Fae, older than the first light. Whispers coil through the Whispering Woods, speaking her name in tongues that taste of ash and memory.

Kaelen's crown grows heavy with unrest as the Unseelie and Seelie courts fracture. Shadows march beneath banners of flame, and the harmony between worlds trembles once more.

As the Veil flickers and the threads of destiny ignite, Elara must decide whether to preserve the fragile peace she forged... or become the fire that remakes it.

Coming Soon:

Book Two of the Veilbound Saga: Embers of the Veil.

Excerpt: Chapter One
The Song Beneath The Ash

The world had been quiet for too long.

Dawn spilled like molten gold over Oakhaven's rooftops, but the light felt brittle, thin, as if the sun itself feared to linger. Elara paused in the garden where the lavender had once sung to her touch. The hum of the Veil, once a steady pulse beneath her skin, now trembled like a wounded heartbeat. Each note of it carried a faint discord she could not name.

The balance she had woven was fraying.

She pressed her palm to the soil, seeking reassurance in the earth's warmth, yet the energy that answered her was restless, whispering of roots that twisted too deep, of shadows stirring in the hollows between worlds.

"You feel it too," Maeve said behind her, voice soft as smoke. The old woman's eyes were clear again, the haze of illness burned away since the Veil had healed. "The silence that isn't silence."

Elara nodded. "It's changing. The Veil breathes differently."

Maeve's gaze drifted toward the forest edge. "Every healing leaves a scar. And sometimes scars remember what caused them."

A chill brushed the morning air. Across the meadow, the line of trees shivered, though no wind moved through them. For an instant, Elara thought she saw the faintest shimmer, a ripple of light and shadow intertwined, and within it, the echo of distant music.

Then it was gone.

That night, sleep eluded her. The dreams that came were fractured, starlit corridors, wings made of glass, Kaelen's silver eyes burning with something she could not read. She woke before dawn to find the hearth cold and the scent of frost heavy in the air.

Outside, a pale mist coiled through the streets of Oakhaven. At its heart, faint footprints glowed like embers fading into ash.

She knelt, touching one. The Veil thrummed in answer, sharp, insistent, almost pained.

Someone, or something, had crossed where no crossing should be.

"Elara."

His voice came from the mist, low and steady, threaded with the same weariness she remembered, and something else beneath it, darker. Kaelen stepped into view, cloak heavy with dew, the light of dawn catching in his hair like liquid silver. He looked older, the weight of his crown etched into the hard line of his jaw.

"You shouldn't be here," she said, though her heart betrayed her with its wild rhythm.

"Nor should they," he replied, glancing toward the forest. "The Seelie are moving. The Veil no longer hides its wounds from them."

Elara's breath caught. "They know?"

"They suspect. And suspicion is enough to start a war."

He drew closer, the air cooling around him. When his gloved hand brushed hers, the Veil's hum steadied for a heartbeat, then flared, alive and warning. Between their palms a spark leapt, faintly golden instead of silver. Both stared at it.

"What was that?" she whispered.

"A resonance I do not understand," he said, voice roughened by awe and fear alike. "The bond between us has changed."

The spark dimmed, leaving the scent of ozone and a whisper in her mind, a voice not her own, distant and desperate: *He wakes beneath the ash.*

Elara recoiled, clutching her temples. Kaelen caught her shoulders. "What did you hear?"

"A warning," she breathed. "Something… ancient."

Kaelen's eyes narrowed, silver gleaming like a blade. "Then the Veil remembers more than we thought."

Above them, clouds gathered where moments ago the sky had been clear. The first drop of rain fell, dark and cold, striking the soil with the scent of smoke. It hissed faintly, as though the world itself burned beneath its skin.

Elara met Kaelen's gaze. "It's beginning again, isn't it?"

He hesitated only a moment before answering, "No, Elara. It never ended."

The wind shifted, carrying a faint, mournful melody, the same haunting tune that had once echoed through the tear in the Veil. It wound through the trees and vanished into the horizon where the realms touched, leaving behind a silence that felt alive.

And in that silence, Elara felt it: a pulse rising from deep within the earth, a gathering of heat like a spark waiting for breath.

The Veil shuddered once. The hum beneath her skin became a flame.

Somewhere beyond sight, the ashes began to glow.

About The Author

Eira Blackthorn writes stories of love entwined with power, shadow, and ancient magic. Her worlds blend romantic intensity with mythic wonder, where every choice carries the weight of destiny, and every heart bears its own kind of magic.

When she isn't writing, Eira can be found beneath stormlit skies, wandering old forests, or scribbling fragments of dialogue on the backs of receipts. She believes every story begins with a question whispered in the dark and answered by a spark of light.

Thorns of the Veil is her debut novel and the first book in **The Veilbound Saga.**

Follow her journeys through the realms through her publishers, MK Storyworks:

📄 **www.mkstoryworks.com**

✦ **Instagram / TikTok / Threads:** @mkstoryworks

About The Publisher

MK Storyworks is a truly global book publisher, dedicated to the timeless mission of connecting compelling authors with enthusiastic readers across the world.

We pride ourselves on curating a diverse and dynamic list that spans the full spectrum of literary interests. Whether you are looking for an immersive escape into a bestselling fiction novel, seeking wisdom and knowledge from groundbreaking non-fiction titles, perfecting a dish with our acclaimed cookbooks, or introducing the magic of reading to the next generation with our enchanting children's books, MK Storyworks delivers stories that inform, entertain, and inspire.

Our commitment to quality, creativity, and global reach ensures that every book we publish finds its place in the hands and hearts of readers, no matter where they are.

Connect with MK Storyworks

Stay up-to-date with our latest releases, author news, and behind-the-scenes glimpses by connecting with us online:

Website: www.mkstoryworks.com

Social Media:

- YouTube: @mkstoryworks
- Instagram: @mkstoryworks
- Facebook: @mkstoryworks
- X: @mkstoryworks
- Pinterest: @mkstoryworks
- TikTok: @mkstoryworks